RAMAKRISHNA PARAMAHANSA

A COMPLETE BIOGRAPHY

RAMAKRISHNA PARAMAHANSA

A COMPLETE BIOGRAPHY

PRADEEP PANDIT

PRABHAT
PRAKASHAN

Published by
PRABHAT PRAKASHAN PVT. LTD.
4/19 Asaf Ali Road,
New Delhi-110 002 (INDIA)
e-mail: prabhatbooks@gmail.com

ISBN 978-93-5562-938-8

RAMAKRISHNA PARAMAHANSA: A COMPLETE BIOGRAPHY
by Pradeep Pandit

Edition
2024

Price
₹ 300 (Rupees Three Hundred only)

Printed at
Sita Fine Arts, Delhi

Author's Note

Why read Ramakrishna Paramahamsa? At first glance, a book on the saint from Dakhineshwar in Paschimbanga may trigger this question.

Multiple explanations can be dished out in answer to the question - one, being that Ramakrishna's teachings help in the resuscitation of religious values in a rather frothy, ephemeral age. It would, however, be erroneous to limit Ramakrishna's contribution to the realms of spirituality alone. More than religious values, what stands out prominently is his emphasis on basic human values at a time when existential angst has burrowed into the human heart like never before. It's here that Ramakrishna's teachings find their core appeal that cuts across a wide cross-section of audience, including the youth.

For all the craving, carping, conniving and shenanigans of the world that have left humankind exhausted of its reserves, the question that Ramakrishna's teachings pose is this: 'ALL THIS BUT FOR WHAT?' The transience of life is but the harshest reality which we have deliberately brushed under the carpet. Perhaps, we are afraid to look reality in the eye and dread facing the fear of uncertainty that envelops the morrow. Worldly contraptions offer momentary respite from the stings of truth. The day we understand the futility of our exercise in our quest for one-upmanship is the day we attain self-realisation. That's the day we begin to channelise our energy in seeking the absolute truth, which in the collective consciousness is called God.

What's best about Ramakrishna's sermons is that they are not sermons at all. At least, they do not appear to be by the way they are expounded. The instances he gives, the anecdotes with which he spices up his spiritual messages are so intimately real that you identify with them. To think that he was born in 1836 in a decrepit village in Bengal, had inconsequential academic grounding and spoke in rustic Bangla, makes it difficult for one to believe that Ramakrishna represents the very core of the spiritual realisation of the seers and sages of India.

Ramakrishna knew that his messages must reach the higher echelons of the Bhadralok community, just as they must percolate down to the unlettered masses. A quietistic saint who founded a universalist and socially active religious movement – a metamorphosis linked to the reformist and proselytizing zeal of his chief disciple, Swami Vivekananda – Ramakrishna displayed a strong streak of pragmatism when it came to explaining his ideas. Precisely the reason why his memory has not been obfuscated by the passage of time even after about 150 years of his death. The simplicity with which he recounted easy-to-relate tales struck an instant chord with his audience.

The greatest contribution of Ramakrishna to the modern world is his message of religious harmony. To him, all religions were the revelation of God in his diverse aspects to satisfy the manifold demands of the human mind. He always insisted that like different photographs of a building taken from different angles, different religions give us the picture of one truth from different points of view. The diverse views are not contradictory, but complementary. Today, with Machiavellians at work to cash in on religious intolerance, Ramakrishna's 'Many Religions, One God' gospel offers a perspective which we need to heed, now more than ever.

The man who initiated no cult arrived at a time when the very foundation of religion and faith in God was crumbling under the relentless blows of materialism and skepticism. Ramakrishna, through his burning spiritual realisation, demonstrated how God resides in each one of us. His amiable approach was shorn of verbosity and religious 'hocus-pocus' which, he knew, could elude the lexicon of a layman. Implicit faith (*bhakti*), he said, is what helps one squeeze through the eye of the needle and attain God-consciousness. Ramakrishna led by example. He lived a simple life with not a shade of conceit in him, though his eccentric mannerisms were occasionally misconstrued.

Ramakrishna attached paramount importance to the youth being initiated on the path of spirituality. "I am merely the initiator," he used to say, "It's the youth who will lead the way to the ultimate truth." He was proud he had a battery of young Turks, like Swami Vivekananda, as his disciples. When a young disciple once asked him if it is proper to get married while trying to know God, Ramakrishna said, "One should try not to. But it's better to get married than rue not tasting the marital soup for the entire life. This could dent his concentration."

This book is an earnest endeavour to bring to the readers a man who lived his own teachings and like a silent force, influences our spiritual thought currents even to this day. Gliding through the pages that bring alive his life and times, one can find solace in his utterances, a serene comfort which is so rare today in the midst of the ripples created by the daily rigmarole of life.

— ***Udayan Mukherjee***

Contents

1

The Beginning

"The closer you come to God, the less you reason or argue. The moment you are united with Him, everything else seizes, arguments and rationalizing. One then goes into a Samadhi – deep meditation – attaining complete silent communion with God."

■ Ramakrishna Paramahamsa

Great men like Guru Nanak, Lord Buddha or Lord Krishna are not born as humans every day. Rarely do stars herald the birth of a divine soul who would affect the Bengal Renaissance during the 19th and 20th centuries. Apart from his stature as *avatar* or God's personification, Ramakrishna Paramahamsa's enduring influence emanates from his pragmatism, his simplicity of thoughts which are not religious encumbrances, but are real and practical.

> *Ramakrishna once said, "My mother was an apotheosis of civility and piety. She was not worldly and forthright. This quality endeared her to the people of the village. My father was an orthodox Brahmin and did not accept gifts from Shudhras."*

On February 18, 1836, Ramakrishna or Gadadhar was born in a quiet village of Kamarpukur in Hoogly - a small district in Bengal. His parents were poor but pious. His father was Khudiram Chattopadhyay and mother, Chandra Devi. They had moved to Kamarpukur in 1814 and settled there permanently. Kamarpukur was a very quiet and tranquil village, surrounded by fields, tall palm trees and greenery. It had a rustic charm quite untouched by the glamour of the city. The permeating peace had a profound influence on Ramakrishna. Pilgrims to Jagannath Puri passed through Kamarpukur.

Ramakrishna's family was extremely generous. His grandfather, Manikram Chattopadhyay was wealthy, according to the existing standards of the time, with 50 acres of land.

Reminiscing about his parents, Ramakrishna once said, "My mother was an apotheosis of civility and piety. She was not worldly and forthright. This quality endeared her to the people of the village. My father was an orthodox Brahmin and did not accept gifts from Shudhras. He would spend most of his time praying to the Lord and singing devotional songs. So deep was his devotion that tears flowed unchecked when he offered his prayers. In his spare time he made garlands for Lord Raghuveer, his family deity."

Ramakrishna's forefathers were from Deraipur village, quite close to Kamarpukur. His grandfather, Manikram Chattopadhyay belonged to a staunch orthodox Brahmin family. However, the family was extremely generous. Manikram was wealthy, according to the existing standards of the time, with 50 acres of land. His practical and humble nature distinguished him. The Chattopadhyay family was popular in the village because of his generous character.

Ramakrishna's father, Khudiram was born in 1775 and had two brothers and a sister. On completion of his formal education from the village school, he got married to Chandra Devi at the age of 24.

Ramakrishna's father, Khudiram was born in 1775 and had two brothers and a sister. On completion of his formal education from the village school, he got married to Chandra Devi at the age of 24. Khudiram had to look after the house when his father died. He had acquired his father's good qualities and dispensed his responsibilities graciously which made him as popular as his father.

They say that money alone doesn't ensure the route to happiness. More than material resources, what brings perfect felicity in a family is trust and dependence on each other. To that end, Chandra Devi, or Chandra as she was fondly called, was a perfect wife, going about her duties with precision and having unflappable faith in the decisions of her husband. She too was as compassionate as Khudiram and soon came to be known as "Maa" in hours of crisis. Nine years after marriage, Chandra Devi was blessed with her first child, a son she named Ramkumar.

Ramanand wanted Khudiram to stand witness to a case as he knew that the latter's reputation would help him win a case in his favour. He knew Khudiram would not agree to be a party to a false case and had to be cajoled to do it.

Life is full of vagaries and a time came when misfortune drove a wedge between Khudiram's happiness. The village zamindar, Ramanand, was a vile man given to corrupt practices, as were most zamindars of the time. Ramanand wanted Khudiram to stand witness to a case as he knew that the latter's reputation would help him win a case in his favour. He knew Khudiram would not agree to be a party to a false case and had to be cajoled to do it.

Khudiram disapproved of being a party to a falsehood which could affect someone's destiny. He was a God-fearing person and despite repeated messages from the zamindar, kept fobbing off the matter. After a lot of dilly-dallying, Khudiram finally garnered the courage to say 'No.'

As expected, Khudiram disapproved of being a party to a falsehood which could affect someone's destiny. He was a God-fearing person and despite repeated messages from the zamindar, kept fobbing off the matter. After a lot of dilly-dallying, Khudiram finally garnered the courage to say 'No.'

That the sledgehammer would fall on Khudiram was anybody's guess. The zamindar was livid and to teach Khudiram a lesson, etched out false documents by dint of which he usurped Khudiram's landed property. He did not even spare his ancestral home. This left Khudiram on the streets, literally. His faith in Lord Raghuveer was, however, never faltered. In fact, it grew stronger with the crisis. His brothers took refuge with their in-laws, but Khudiram had nowhere to go. It was then that a friend, Sukhram Goswami suggested that he leave Beruipur and shift base to Kamarpukur to begin life afresh.

The zamindar was livid and to teach Khudiram a lesson, etched out false documents by dint of which he usurped Khudiram's landed property. He did not even spare his ancestral home. This left Khudiram on the streets, literally.

Sukhram, who was a zamindar, wasn't like the rest of the ilk. He was compassionate and his love for his village was well-known. He invited Khudiram and accommodated him in one portion of his palatial house. Misfortune, however, struck again and Sukhram passed away in 1824. His passing away saw his ancestral house being reduced to ruins until it was sold off to Laha family.

At the age of 39, Khudiram, along with his wife and two kids, laid the foundation stone of his new house in Kamarpukur. Adversity had failed to make him cringe and his faith in the Almighty paid off. The society was gradually metamorphosing, for the worse, unfortunately. Double-speak and cynicism were slowly spreading their tentacles. All this did not hamper Khudiram's progress. Not merely a house, he also managed to get half-an-acre of land for himself, that too, one that was eminently fertile.

> *Realising he had been ordained by the Lord, he dug up the ground at a little distance from the tree as instructed and found an idol of Raghuveer. A serpent guarding the idol slowly moved away as if satisfied that the idol had fallen into the safe hands of an able caretaker.*

Then came a turning point in Khudiram's life. While returning from a sojourn to a nearby village, he fell asleep under a tree. Lord Raghuveer arrived in his dream and said, "I am tired of being here. Take me to your house." "But my Lord, despite being a devotee, I am too poor to even think of taking you to my house," Khudiram pleaded. At this stage, he was jolted out of his slumber. Realising he had been ordained by the Lord, he dug up the ground at a little distance from the tree as instructed and found an idol of Raghuveer. A serpent guarding the idol slowly moved away as if satisfied that the idol had fallen into the safe hands of an able caretaker.

> *Ramkumar had foretold that his wife would pass away after delivering her first baby and that is exactly what happened. He was 35 when his wife gave birth to a son and left for heavenly abode.*

The deity's presence made Khudiram a household name. His love and devotion for the Lord was much talked about. He soon became the cynosure of the villagers who showered their respect on him and his family. Chandra Devi, too, came to be known as someone who would go the whole hog to help anyone who needed her assistance.

Six years after settling in Kamarpukur, Khudiram got his son, Ramkumar and his daughter married. Ramkumar, by then, had agreed to assist his father in managing the household affairs. He had foretold that his wife would pass away after delivering her first baby and that is exactly what happened. Ramkumar was 35 when his wife gave birth to a son and left for heavenly abode. With Ramkumar taking up all household responsibilities, Khudiram decided to go on a pilgrimage.

Khudiram's first destination was Rameshwaram which he traversed on foot. In 1826 Khudiram become a father to a son whom he named Rameshwar. In 1835, he went to Gaya, again on foot. He offered his tributes to his forefathers there. It was here that he had a dream in which Lord Gadadhara (a form of Lord Vishnu) said that he would be born as his son. Far away in Kamarpukur, almost at the same time, Chandra Devi also experienced a vision of light entering her womb from Lord Shiva's temple. On returning from Gaya, Khudiram, who was now 60, found Chandra a changed woman. She had become more docile and draped in humility that was reminiscent of a divine

Khudiram's first destination was Rameshwaram which he traversed on foot. In 1826 Khudiram become a father to a son whom he named Rameshwar. In 1835, he went to Gaya, again on foot.

presence within her. He listened to the strange experience his wife had had.

The morning of February 18, 1836 heralded the moment. Ramkrishna's birth seemed to have adorned nature with unbound joy. Spring came in full bloom, birds sang and flowers never smelled more pleasant. Astrologers predicted that the destiny of the human race was inextricably linked to the child. The child was named Gadadhar who would grow up to be known the world over as Sri Sri Ramakrishna Paramahamsa.

Astrologers predicted that the destiny of the human race was inextricably linked to the child. The child was named Gadadhar who would grow up to be known the world over as Sri Sri Ramakrishna Paramahamsa.

Some children are so precocious that they soon make their way into the hearts of people. With a sharp mind, Gadadhar was quick on the uptake. He would remember what he had read to the last letter, be it mythological tales or the epics. Even the relatively difficult subjects were not difficult for him to comprehend.

The mother in Chandra was worried. Gadadhar's antics provoked concern. Sometimes, he would be as light as a kid. At times, he would weigh so heavy that Chandra could not lift him alone. Khudiram would constantly comfort his wife that they had an *avatar* as their son and such strange characteristics were only normal.

To provide some diversion to the little Gadadhar, he was enrolled with a village school run by the Laha family. The Lahas revered Khudiram and had arranged for a grand *annaprasana* ceremony after Gadadhar's birth. Gadadhar soon began to master his lessons in school. The only subject he would fight shy of was Mathematics. He even learnt to make idols of Gods and Goddesses from a *kumhar* (potter). Gadadhar's solemn nature made him stand out from the rest of the folks. He was serious about everything and extremely honest when it came to

Gadadhar soon began to master his lessons in school. The only subject he would fight shy of was Mathematics. He even learnt to make idols of Gods and Goddesses from a kumhar (potter).

admitting mistakes. As is wont of kids, they tend to camouflage their mistakes with lies for fear of punishment. Not Gadadhar, though. He would admit to his mistakes in all humility and swear never to make them again. His forthrightness and gentility made him immensely popular.

Gadadhar's first brush with *samadhi* (trance) was at the ripe age of six. It is said that while walking along the paddy fields, a flock of white cranes flying against a backdrop of dark thunderous clouds caught his vision. He reportedly became so absorbed by this scene that he lost consciousness and experienced indescribable joy in that state. "I can't describe the spiritual ecstasy in words at that moment," he recalled later.

Gadadhar's first brush with samadhi (trance) was at the ripe age of six. It is said that while walking along the paddy fields, a flock of white cranes flying against a backdrop of dark thunderous clouds caught his vision.

Tragedy struck at the age of seven with the passing away of his father. Khudiram's loss was a colossal setback. It was for the first time Gadadhar realised life's transient nature. This realisation made him dig deeper into religious books and confabulate with *sadhus* who would stop at Kamarpukur *en route* to Puri. With the sacred thread ceremony at the age of nine, Gadadhar was initiated into meditation.

Gadadhar formed his own group and staged plays, mostly based on the Ramayana and the Mahabharata. Tales based on Radha and Krishna, were his favourites.

Once during *Shivratri*, a play was being staged in the village where the person who was to portray the character of Lord Shiva fell sick. Gadadhar was requested to play the part. When he was dressed up in the Lord's attire, the audience was awestruck. It was as if the Lord had descended on the earth. Later, people came to know that Gadadhar had gone into a trance while playing the part on stage.

Since then, Gadadhar formed his own group and staged plays, mostly based on the *Ramayana* and the *Mahabharata.* Tales based on Radha and Krishna, were his favourites. He would usually play a role in such plays, that of Radha or Lord Krishna and the audience would subsequently be wowed by his adeptness in essaying the roles. The high point in the plays came each time he went into a trance. Amid all this, his penchant for school started waning.

Gadadhar was growing up to be quite a youth, handsome, with curly locks of hair, fair complexion and sparkling eyes. In 1849, Ramkumar went to Kolkata (then Calcutta) to look for better avenues to improve his finances. Once there, he opened a Sanskrit Academy to divert Gadadhar's attention towards studies. However, Gadadhar's heart lay in religious activities. Soon, he would be invited to perform *pujas* on auspicious occasions. His *pujas* would be shorn away from what traditional pundits would do. He would pray for hours, sing and cry in front of the deities. His devotion paved his way to carve a place in the hearts

He would pray for hours, sing and cry in front of the deities. His devotion paved his way to carve a place in the hearts of the devotees. Conventional studies now seemed a far too distant cause for Gadadhar.

of the devotees. Conventional studies now seemed a far too distant cause for Gadadhar.

Much to Ramkumar's chagrin, Gadadhar was increasingly being consumed by a happy-go-lucky attitude. Ramkumar wanted him to appreciate worldly matters for a smooth future. He advised his sibling to pay some attention to studies as well. "What for?" would be Gadadhar's repartee. "Merely to earn a livelihood? But my quest is for none less than eternal satisfaction."

Ramkumar wanted him to appreciate worldly matters for a smooth future. He advised his sibling to pay some attention to studies as well. "What for?" would be Gadadhar's repartee. "Merely to earn a livelihood? But my quest is for none less than eternal satisfaction."

In those days, there lived an affluent widow in Kolkata by the name of Rani Rashmoni. Born a *shudra*, her courage, intellect and religious beliefs were exemplary. She bought some 20 acres of land on the eastern side of the Ganges at Dakhineshwar and built a huge temple of Goddess Kali on it, the gates of which were thrown open to the public on May 31, 1855. The campus also housed Shiva, Radha-Krishna and Vishnu temples. The main attraction was, however, the Kali temple which till date attracts thousands of pilgrims daily from all over the world.

Gadadhar came to Dakhineshwar with Ramkumar, where the latter was entrusted with the duty of the chief priest of the Kali temple. Gadadhar, who was initially too homesick, gradually found himself being attracted to the rituals of the temple. Rani Rashmoni's son-in-law, Mathur Babu, who was a patron of the temple, knew about Gadadhar's trances and wanted him to take more interest in the temple rituals. But Gadadhar was somehow reluctant. Mathur Babu waited for an opportune moment when Gadadhar could be persuaded.

The moment came with the arrival of Gadadhar's cousin, Hriday from Sihore near Kamarpukur. Gadadhar was elated to see his childhood friend. Hriday was looking for a job. Gadadhar thought of a plan. He told Mathur Babu that he would agree to participate in the rituals, provided Hriday was allowed to assist him. Mathur Babu readily acquiesced.

Gadadhar left everyone stunned with his remark, "If your son-in-law were to fracture a leg, would you treat his injured leg or go hunting for another son-in-law? Obviously, you would have him treated. So, mend the idol's leg and worship the Lord again." Rani Rashmoni smiled. She was relieved.

One day, it so happened that the priest in charge of the Radhakant temple accidentally broke a leg of the idol of Lord Krishna. There was a hue and cry and it was suggested that the idol be replaced immediately as broken idols were considered inauspicious. Rani Rashmoni thought it prudent to take Gadadhar's opinion. Not one to mince words, Gadadhar left everyone stunned with his remark, "If your son-in-law were to fracture a leg, would you treat his injured leg or go hunting for another son-in-law? Obviously, you would have him treated. So, mend the idol's leg and worship the Lord again." Rani Rashmoni smiled. She was relieved. From then on, Gadadhar was appointed the Priest of the Radhakant temple.

Mantras or holy hymns were not alien to Gadadhar. He knew most of them by rote. The way he mouthed the *mantras* were far removed from the stereotypical ways the traditional pundits said them. When he prayed at the Radhakant temple, he would often go into trances. Ramkumar wanted Gadadhar to learn Goddess Kali's *mantras* as well. The first *mantra* stunned him into silence and tears streamed down his eyes incessantly. He then shrieked as if struck by lightning and went into a trance. Mathur Babu knew Gadadhar was ready, eventually. He was given the additional responsibility of the Kali temple.

In 1856, Ramkumar, the man whom Gadadhar regarded no less than his father, passed away.

❑

2

Tryst with 'Maa Kali'

"The fish may be far away. Yet, when an attractive bait is thrown into the pond, the fish hastily rises to grab it. Similarly, God quickly approaches the devotee whose heart is full of devotion and faith. That's the bait for Him."

By the time he was 20, Ramakrishna had become the head priest of the Kali temple. As time went by, Rani Rashmoni, who lived with four of her daughters, grew increasingly fond of him. Rashmoni's third daughter was married to Mathurnath Biswas or Mathur Babu who assisted his mother-in-law in the administration of the temple affairs. Rashmoni, following the death of her husband, Rajchandra Das, spent most of her days in pilgrimage. She once had a dream where she was asked to build a temple of Goddess Kali. Thus Dakhineshwar Kalibari came into being and Ramakrishna became the head priest. This was destined to be and Ramakrishna carved a niche in Rashmoni's heart not by dint of his *puja*, but by his unwavering faith in the Goddess.

The place where Panchwati stands today was once full of dense, thorny bushes and ghosts were believed to reside there. Ramakrishna did not dread the supernatural and went amid the bushes to meditate. Hriday tried to dissuade him, but to no avail. Hriday made ominous noises, threw stones at Ramakrishna to intimidate him, but his tricks fell flat. Ramakrishna was undeterred in his resolve.

Hours on end ticked by as Ramakrishna meditated amid the bushes. He would go there in the night and come back in the morning. His eyes would be swollen due to crying. While meditating, he would put all his clothes aside, even his sacred thread. He is said to have told Hriday, "While praying to the Almighty, one must detach himself from everything that even remotely reminds him of his own self." Hriday often failed to understand the import of such statements, but his loyalty to Ramakrishna never faltered.

> *One night, Hriday decided to seek the answers for himself. He would often wonder what Ramakrishna does behind the bushes and why all his activities were nocturnal. Garnering all his strength, he made it to the bushes and saw Ramakrishna deep in meditation, his clothes and sacred thread by his side.*

One night, Hriday decided to seek the answers for himself. He would often wonder what Ramakrishna does behind the bushes and why all his activities were nocturnal. Garnering all his strength, he made it to the bushes and saw Ramakrishna deep in meditation, his clothes and sacred thread by his side. "What are you doing here? Aren't you aware that the sacred thread should never be removed?" Hriday asked the question time and again, but could not elicit a reply. Sometime later, when Ramakrishna awoke from his trance, he said, "I was meditating. All I had in my mind was Maa Kali. You see, meditation is done without remembering anything. If you remember anything other than what you are focusing on, you are lost." The import of the statement was lost on Hriday again.

Ramakrishna's mannerisms became all the more unpredictable by the day. In the midst of decorating the Mother with flowers, he would throw the flowers on himself. He would suddenly break into tears, scrub his face on the ground and cry insolubly. The only refrain one could hear from him was "Maa..."

Meanwhile, Ramakrishna's mannerisms became all the more unpredictable by the day. In the midst of decorating the Mother with flowers, he would throw the flowers on himself. He would suddenly break into tears, scrub his face on the ground and cry insolubly. The only refrain one could hear from him was "Maa..." He would go into an *advaita* (non-dual) trance and become one with the Goddess. As the trance came, he would utter, "Maa, You are me, I am You." Ramakrishna's routine went haywire. He could no longer carry out his duties as the head priest. For hours on end, he would sit in front of the Goddess, sobbing and indulging in soliloquy. "Why am I not able to see you? Are you for real or just a figment of the imagination?" he would constantly ask Goddess Kali. Food and sleep consequently went for a toss.

He would go into an advaita (non-dual) trance and become one with the Goddess. As the trance came, he would utter, "Maa, You are me, I am You." Ramakrishna's routine went haywire. He could no longer carry out his duties as the head priest.

Whenever Ramakrishna felt a surge of feelings deep within, he would listen to the devotional songs of Ramprasad and Kamalakant, two of Bengal's musical wordsmiths whose lyrics touched the innermost chord of the heart with vivid descriptions of Goddess Kali. Ramakrishna would listen to the songs and cry aloud, "Hey Maa, your *darshan* enabled Ramprasad to write such thoughtful words in your glory. Am I so unfortunate that I shall never be able to see you?"

Ramakrishna would listen to the songs and cry aloud, "Hey Maa, your darshan enabled Ramprasad to write such thoughtful words in your glory. Am I so unfortunate that I shall never be able to see you?"

Not for long could the Goddess ignore the wailings of her son. Ramakrishna later described his first *darshan* of Goddess Kali thus: "I was feeling so impatient without the divine *darshan* of Maa. Life had become so meaningless. I felt like a wet towel being wrung dry. There was a sword dangling from the wall at the temple and I decided to end my life with it. As I lifted the sword to decapitate myself,

I suddenly felt the walls, ceiling and everything around me in the temple, disappear. I was facing a vast ocean, whose high tides with thunderous shrieks were rising to engulf me. I knew not what was happening outside, but deep within I felt a new calm descending on me, as if I were drenched in divine benediction. As I lost consciousness, I felt the presence of Maa Kali." When Ramakrishna regained consciousness after a while, the only word that played on his lips was "Maa".

Ramakrishna simply couldn't forget his first brush with Maa Kali, even if it were momentary. Time and again, he could be seen imploring the Goddess for another darshan.

Ramakrishna simply couldn't forget his first brush with Maa Kali, even if it were momentary. Time and again, he could be seen imploring the Goddess for another *darshan*. His mannerisms became more erratic, to the extent that while some called the act an unmitigated sham, others held it up for ridicule. His trances became longer.

Regular rituals came to a near-halt. He was hassled by his joint pain. Had it not been for Hriday's constant care, Ramakrishna couldn't have carried on for long.

Criticism became shriller, but those in his defence never let him alone and they boldly faced all flak. They answered all those who lampooned him. The society is usually short-sighted, seldom able to look beyond the obvious. Ramakrishna was above the ordinary, unfettered by the norms of society. He neither ate nor drank. He was beginning to see God in everyone – he could spot Sita in a prostitute and Krishna in a British. Actually, these were pointers that he was gradually becoming one with the Almighty. He was

He was beginning to see God in everyone – he could spot Sita in a prostitute and Krishna in a British. Actually, these were pointers that he was gradually becoming one with the Almighty. He was Rama, he was Kali, he was Krishna, he was Radha and he was Hanumana. The transformation was complete.

Rama, he was Kali, he was Krishna, he was Radha and he was Hanumana. The transformation was complete.

When some people suggested that he was sick and should go for treatment, he agreed to do so. Acceptance had become him. There wasn't a trace of arrogance for having seen the Almighty. He knew that God was for real and thus had no arguments to offer. He gladly accepted both acceptance and rejection of his views.

Many in this generation would take this as utter nonsense, but the fact of 'So-ham' (He is me) remains. It is the process of entering the realms of divinity. What comes with it is disarming simplicity and that's what characterised Ramakrishna. He was so simple in his demeanour that he readily accepted other points of view. When some people suggested that he was sick and should go for treatment, he agreed to do so. Acceptance had become him. There wasn't a trace of arrogance for having seen the Almighty. He knew that God was for real and thus had no arguments to offer. He gladly accepted both acceptance and rejection of his views.

First, he felt Her presence. Then, he felt Her touch. He would increasingly utter, "Maa said that..." Since Ramakrishna would no longer be able to do the daily rituals, his cousin Haladhari was made the priest. A staunch orthodox when it came to following rituals, Haladhari wasn't quite impressed with Ramakrishna. After all, God's presence is to be felt, which is far greater than simply following rituals. One changes the Almighty's clothes, offers *naibaidya* (food). One can either do it as a matter of routine or can become one while dispensing with his duties. It's clearly a matter of the heart.

First, he felt Her presence. Then, he felt Her touch. He would increasingly utter, "Maa said that..." Since Ramakrishna would no longer be able to do the daily rituals, his cousin Haladhari was made the priest. A staunch orthodox when it came to following rituals, Haladhari wasn't quite impressed with Ramakrishna.

Ramakrishna's faith was above mundane earthly arguments. Hriday stands testimony to this.

Hriday said his fears were two-pronged: one, he was a traditional Brahmin and couldn't quite digest what he saw and two, he was afraid that Rani Rashmoni and Mathur Babu would take a dim view of Ramakrishna's antics.

He would often say that watching Ramakrishna pray inspired awe in the onlookers. His offerings were as unconventional as they were formidable. He would first offer flowers to himself and then to Goddess Kali. Hriday said his fears were two-pronged: one, he was a traditional Brahmin and couldn't quite digest what he saw and two, he was afraid that Rani Rashmoni and Mathur Babu would take a dim view of Ramakrishna's antics. As time went by, Hriday realised that he was separated from his cousin by a gulf of divergent views - he had learnt through tradition and Ramakrishna through practice. This realisation fortified Hriday's faith in his cousin.

Hriday may have been convinced of Ramakrishna's selfless devotion, but this was not the case with a crop of detractors who abhorred the ascetic's ways. Flowers offered to himself and then to Kali, *prasada* eaten and then offered to the Goddess – all these were considered sacrilegious. The temple management was first informed and soon enough, the word reached Mathur Babu. Known for his equanimity, Mathur Babu promised to check it out for himself and made a surprise visit to the temple to uncover the truth behind the allegations. Ramakrishna was then lost in his prayers, oblivious that he was being watched. Mathur Babu stood transfixed. Never before had he seen such unstained devotion. He quietly returned and sent a word to the temple management that Ramakrishna's

Known for his equanimity, Mathur Babu promised to check it out for himself and made a surprise visit to the temple to uncover the truth behind the allegations. Ramakrishna was then lost in his prayers, oblivious that he was being watched. Mathur Babu stood transfixed. Never before had he seen such unstained devotion.

antics, that many found objectionable, were the result of his selfless devotion to the Goddess. Having reached such a level, such out-of-the-ordinary mannerisms were only natural. Mathur Babu specified that Ramakrishna not be impeded in any way from carrying out his prayers the way he did.

Bhakti, it is believed, are of two varieties – one, that of a traditionalist who follows holy scriptures and two, that of one whose sole route to the Lord is his selfless love.

Bhakti, it is believed, are of two varieties – one, that of a traditionalist who follows holy scriptures and two, that of one whose sole route to the Lord is his selfless love. It is accepted that there are five ways *pujas* are performed. The first is calm meditation, the one followed by hermits. The second is complete surrender to the Lord. The third is acceptance of the Lord as your *sakha* (friend). The fourth is *vatsalya*, where the devotee considers himself as a child and the Lord as his guardian. The fifth form of *puja* is *madhurya*, where the Lord and the devotee are seen as lovers.

Ramakrishna, more than any other ascetic, experimented with all the five ways. His constant preoccupation with Goddess Kali had sheared him away from worldly matters. Stories about his mannerisms reached Kamarpukur and his mother, Chandra, who was still alive, grew anxious. Villagers suggested that Ramakrishna be made to tie the nuptial knot as the onus of conjugal life will compel him to accept domestic responsibilities. He was advised to take a break and go home as he was sick and needed rest. Ramakrishna offered no objections. He was more than happy to accept the suggestion. "If you say I am sick, well, I will go home and take some rest," pat came the reply with no trace of indignation. Once home, his marriage was solemnized with Shardamani Devi or Sharda Maa in 1859. Sharda Maa was barely five at that time.

Villagers suggested that Ramakrishna be made to tie the nuptial knot as the onus of conjugal life will compel him to accept domestic responsibilities. He was advised to take a break and go home as he was sick and needed rest.

Child marriage was prevalent in those times. But it was more a solemn union of two souls than anything physical. The girl used to go back to her parents after marriage and would return after eight or nine years following a ceremony. Sharda Maa too went back to her parents and Ramakrishna returned to Dakhineshwar. However, contrary to expectations, his antics, far from fading away, only became more pronounced.

Mathur Babu was in a quandary – at times he felt Ramakrishna was going unhinged and at times, he felt he had found inner peace by unraveling the mystery of nature, precisely the reason why people were jealous of him.

Mathur Babu was in a quandary – at times he felt Ramakrishna was going unhinged and at times, he felt he had found inner peace by unraveling the mystery of nature, precisely the reason why people were jealous of him.

Mathur Babu once gifted an expensive *shawl* to Ramakrishna. He even emphasized that it cost him a good Rs 1,000, a princely sum then.

Ramakrishna was ecstatic. His joy was more akin to a child and in keeping with his childlike innocence, he would show the *shawl* to everyone and even quote the price. After some time, his attitude changed. He kept thinking that what an expensive *shawl* can do in preventing the chill from affecting the body, an ordinary quilt can do as much. In fact, he reasoned that such an expensive *shawl* only instilled a false sense of arrogance in a person. "Will this *shawl* bring me any closer to Maa Kali?" he would ask himself. It was only a matter of time that he discarded the *shawl,* threw it on the ground and even spat on it.

He kept thinking that what an expensive shawl can do in preventing the chill from affecting the body, an ordinary quilt can do as much. "Will this shawl bring me any closer to Maa Kali?" he would ask himself. It was only a matter of time that he discarded the shawl, threw it on the ground and even spat on it.

There was another occasion when Rani Rashmoni and Mathur Babu mistook

Ramakrishna's antics as his craving for sexual gratification. They sent some prostitutes to force him out of his trance. Needless to say, the efforts failed and Ramakrishna ended up seeing the visage of Goddess Kali in the prostitutes, thus shaming them into repentance.

Swami Shraddhanandaji, a saint who propagated the teachings of Ramakrishna Paramahamsa and Swami Vivekananda, offers an interesting insight into Ramakrishna's marriage. He says marriages in those days meant household chores for a woman. Ramakrishna never intended the same for Sharda Maa. He agreed to marriage to show the world the resolve to abstain from sexual desires even with the presence of one's wife. He taught Sharda Maa many lessons in life, worshipped her as the Goddess and catapulted the concept of marriage to a celestial echelon.

❑

3

Experiments with Truth

"Divine reality is a limitless ocean of consciousness and individual awareness is a jar."

A popular saying goes that one who has sunk has plumbed the depths of the sea, the swimmer is oblivious of it. Ramkrishna had plumbed the deepest recesses of meditation. That's what made him a Paramahamsa. His words and statements, therefore, acquired a different plane. Ramakrishna's father, Khudiram, was a staunch devotee of Lord Rama. It is accepted that in terms of devotion to his master, no one has ever exceeded Lord Hanumana. Ramakrishna wanted to test how it feels to follow Hanumana. He lived on trees, ate fruits and pranced around just the way a monkey would. "It was a strange experience for me," Ramakrishna recalled later. "My personality underwent a sea change. I wasn't the same any more. My spinal cord lengthened by about an inch and came back to its normal size only after I resumed my usual routine."

Deep meditation tags along experiences of the strangest kind. Ramakrishna remembers that he was once sitting at the Panchwati, when suddenly he saw a blinding spray of light approaching him. The light gave way to a woman who didn't quite look earthly. She was still approaching Ramakrishna when a monkey came out of nowhere and sat by her side. It was then that Ramakrishna realised that the woman was Mother Sita. He was about to fall at her feet when She possessed him throwing him into a trance.

All of a sudden, Ramakrishna stopped and slapped Rashmoni twice. "Thinking of material gains here too?" admonished Ramakrishna. While several onlookers protested, Rashmoni humbly admitted to her mistake. "I was indeed thinking about a court matter," was her admittance.

There are beatific experience often inspired by meditation, many of which even science has failed to spurn. There is an instance when Rani Rashmoni came to Dakhineshwar for a dip into the Ganges. While she sat for a *puja*, she requested Ramakrishna to sing a devotional song. Ramakrishna began and all of a sudden stopped after a while and slapped Rashmoni twice. A petrified silence descended on the temple. "Thinking of material gains here too?" admonished Ramakrishna. While several onlookers protested,

Rashmoni humbly admitted to her mistake. "I was indeed thinking about a court matter," was her admittance.

> *The sanyasin readily agreed to meet him. Once face-to-face, both their eyes welled up with tears. "My child, I knew you were there somewhere on the banks of the Ganges," said the sanyasin. "Maa, how did you know about me?" asked Ramakrishna. Actually, both were devotees of Goddess Kali.*

While sitting on the banks of the *Ganges* one day, Ramakrishna noticed a *sanyasin* (lady ascetic), possibly in her forties, coming on a boat. She had a handful of books kept on her lap. Something about the lady made Ramakrishna impatient from deep within. He couldn't contain himself, went back to his room and asked Hriday to ask the *sanyasin* to meet him. Hriday was a bit shocked. Never had Ramakrishna shown such interest in a woman. He went over to the woman and expressed his cousin's wish. The *sanyasin* readily agreed to meet him. Once face-to-face, both their eyes welled up with tears. "My child, I knew you were there somewhere on the banks of the *Ganges*," said the *sanyasin*. "Maa, how did you know about me?" asked Ramakrishna. Actually, both were devotees of Goddess Kali.

Ramakrishna related his experiences to the sanyasin. He told, how his mannerisms had become the butt of jokes. "People call me mad. Am I really mad?" he kept asking repeatedly. The sanyasin listened patiently, as patiently as a mother would. "No, my child. You aren't mad. People are ignorant. Such experiences are called 'mahabhav' in our holy scriptures.

Ramakrishna related his experiences to the *sanyasin*. He told him how his mannerisms had become the butt of jokes. "People call me mad. Am I really mad?" he kept asking repeatedly. The *sanyasin* listened patiently, as patiently as a mother would. "No, my child. You aren't mad. People are ignorant. Such experiences are called *'mahabhav'* in our holy scriptures. Whoever accepts the Almighty with the love and devotion that you have, must traverse the same path. Only Radha and Gaurang have had such experiences," she comforted Ramakrishna.

> *"Whom I saw in my trance, I saw him right in front of me when I came out of it," said the sanyasin. She then immersed the idol of Lord Raghuveer into the Ganges. She didn't need him anymore. She had found her Lord. She had seen Lord Rama in Ramakrishna.*

The *sanyasin* had an idol of Lord Raghuveer. She would cook her own food and offer it to her Lord first. As she was cooking at the Panchwati, Ramakrishna, who was in his room, felt someone was calling him. He went over to the Panchwati and found the *sanyasin* offering food to Lord Raghuveer. As if possessed by an unknown force, Ramakrishna took the food and started eating. When the *sanyasin* opened her eyes, she saw Ramakrishna devouring the food meant for her Lord. By then, Ramakrishna had gone into a trance. After a while, when he came to his senses, he felt ashamed of his conduct and asked for her forgiveness. "Whom I saw in my trance, I saw him right in front of me when I came out of it," said the *sanyasin*. She then immersed the idol of Lord Raghuveer into the *Ganges*. She didn't need him anymore. She had found her Lord. She had seen Lord Rama in Ramakrishna.

Mathur Babu was resting in his room one day when he noticed Ramakrishna strolling and chanting the hymns of Lord Shiva. Almost involuntarily, tears streaked down his cheeks. After a while, he ran over to Ramakrishna and fell at his feet. Ramakrishna was aghast.

Mathur Babu was resting in his room one day when he noticed Ramakrishna strolling and chanting the hymns of Lord Shiva. Almost involuntarily, tears streaked down his cheeks. After a while, he ran over to Ramakrishna and fell at his feet. Ramakrishna was aghast. "What are you doing? What will people say if they see Rani Rashmoni's son-in-law at the feet of an ascetic?" reasoned Ramakrishna. To this, Mathur Babu said, "As I watched you walk up towards me, I saw Goddess

Kali and as you walked further away, you were Lord Shiva. First I thought I was imagining things, but each time I saw you, I had the same vision." Ramakrishna replied all too innocently, "Well Sir, I wasn't in my senses then, you see. I don't know what was happening to me."

With the arrival of winter, Rani Rashmoni fell ill. She never recuperated and passed away on February 20, 1869. All responsibilities of her vast property fell on Mathur Babu's shoulders. He would always say that whatever he has belonged to Ramakrishna and he was merely a follower. Ramakrishna was never too mild on Mathur Babu when it came to mistakes. He would chide him time and again, but Mathur Babu did not take any umbrage. He kept serving Maa Kali and

Ramakrishna was never too mild on Mathur Babu when it came to mistakes. He would chide him time and again, but Mathur Babu did not take any umbrage. He kept serving Maa Kali and would say in Ramakrishna's glory, "He hails from a country where the night never descends."

would say in Ramakrishna's glory, "He hails from a country where the night never descends."

Conceit or disdain was one trait that was strikingly missing in Ramakrishna despite all that he had achieved at a relatively young age. He also believed that *parashakti* (supreme, divine power) was an impediment to attaining oneness with the Almighty as it creates delusions of power which in turns impedes the union. There is an incident involving Bhairavi who had brought along Chandra and Girija Devi to Ramakrishna. Both Chandra and Girija had acquired huge powers, but somehow found that certain answers were eluding them. Ramakrishna often made fun of such powers. To corroborate his point, he often recounted a story of two brothers, which he related to Chandra and Girija Devi too. The story went thus: There once lived two brothers. The elder became an ascetic and practised penance for 12 years, acquiring great powers in the process. The younger brother became a family person, took up a good job and was well-settled in life. One day, the elder brother came along to meet the younger brother. While they spoke on the banks of a river, the younger brother asked, "What have you achieved after 12 years of rigorous penance?" Waiting impatiently to display his acquired prowess, the elder brother said a few mantras and started walking on the river until he went over to the other side. "What do you say?" he asked with pride. The younger brother smiled, called a boat, gave half-an-*anna* to the boatman and asked him to ferry him to the other end of the river. "You see," he told his elder brother, "What took you 12 years to achieve, took me half-an-*anna* to get the same." The elder brother knew he had wasted his time in his quest for supreme powers and was as far from God as he was before. He vowed to begin his *sadhna*

The elder brother said a few mantras and started walking on the river until he went over to the other side. "What do you say?" he asked with pride. The younger brother smiled, called a boat, gave half-an-anna to the boatman and asked him to ferry him to the other end of the river. "You see," he told his elder brother, "What took you 12 years to achieve, took me half-an-anna to get the same."

(meditation) in all austerity, this time to be one with God.

> *The ascetic was waiting for just that question. "I will show you," he said. "Do you see the elephant there? Watch." He chanted some mantras and the huge animal collapsed on the ground, lifeless. "Now watch closely again," said the ascetic. He chanted a few more mantras and the tusker was back on its feet, alive and kicking.*

There was another pet anecdote that Ramkrishna often regaled his audience with. There was an ascetic who had acquired *'vak siddhi'* (the power by which whatever you say turns out to be true). He once came across a *sadhu* who was constantly chanting the name of God. After listening to him for some time, the ascetic, asked him, "What will this non-stop chirping help you achieve?" "But I want to achieve nothing. The Lord's name keeps playing on my lips and that's what gives me the hope that it will someday bring me that much closer to Him," the *sadhu* said. The ascetic wasn't convinced. "But this will help you achieve nothing," he said. "What have you achieved?" asked the *sadhu*. The ascetic was waiting for just that question. "I will show you," he said. "Do you see the elephant there? Watch." He chanted some *mantras* and the huge animal collapsed on the ground, lifeless. "Now watch closely again," said the ascetic. He chanted a few more *mantras* and the tusker was back on its feet, alive and kicking. "That's achievement, you see," said the ascetic with an air of authority. "Really?" questioned the *sadhu*. "But what have you achieved? Have you been able to win over life and death? Have your powers brought you even a shred closer to God?" The ascetic fell mum. He understood.

"That's achievement, you see," said the ascetic with an air of authority. "Really?" questioned the sadhu. "But what have you achieved? Have you been able to win over life and death? Have your powers brought you even a shred closer to God?" The ascetic fell mum. He understood.

Bhairavi lived on at Dakhineshwar for a long time, looking after Ramakrishna like her own son. An accomplished *tantric* in her own right, she would offer her remedies and advice to Ramakrishna in times of crisis. Once when Ramakrishna fell sick with acute headache and burning sensation all over the body, Bhairavi read somewhere in the holy scriptures that Radha and Chaitanya too had to pass through such excruciating pain. She read about how smearing the body with sandal paste could bring in some relief. She did that and Ramakrishna's pain subsided. On another occasion, Ramakrishna's appetite increased manifold. He would devour a lot of

Once when Ramakrishna fell sick with acute headache and burning sensation all over the body, Bhairavi read somewhere in the holy scriptures that Radha and Chaitanya too had to pass through such excruciating pain. She read about how smearing the body with sandal paste could bring in some relief. She did that and Ramakrishna's pain subsided.

food and still feel hungry. Bhairavi would comfort him, saying, "Chastening of the five senses takes time, my child. So, don't worry. This will pass." She instructed the cooks to prepare variegated delicacies for Ramakrishna, which the latter ate with delight. Gradually, the gargantuan appetite wore thin and in a few days, Ramakrishna was his usual self.

Bhairavi would comfort him, saying, "Chastening of the five senses takes time, my child. So, don't worry. This will pass." She instructed the cooks to prepare variegated delicacies for Ramakrishna, which the latter ate with delight. Gradually, the gargantuan appetite wore thin and in a few days, Ramakrishna was his usual self.

A turning point in Ramakrishna's life came with the arrival of famous Vedanta scholar, Digambar Totapuri in Dakhineshwar. Ramakrishna was lost in his thoughts on the stairs of the Kali temple when Totapuri, a wanderer by nature, arrived on the scene. The radiance in

Ramakrishna's visage held him spellbound. He found himself saying, "My child, you have gone far on the path of truth. But your quest isn't over yet. I can impart the knowledge of *Vedanta, shastra* which will be of great help to you." Ramakrishna wouldn't do anything without prior permission from Maa Kali. Permission granted, he began his lessons. As time went by, his faith deepened and he was, as he said himself, "Introduced to the limitless, infinite and effulgent ocean of consciousness." Totapuri's teachings were based on complete detachment, the total surrender of the self. Ramakrishna later said that detachment from 'form' and 'name' and subsequently merging with the soul at times seemed an impossible exercise. But Totapuri was recalcitrant. He had unwavering faith in his disciple.

Ramakrishna wouldn't do anything without prior permission from Maa Kali. Permission granted, he began his lessons. As time went by, his faith deepened and he was, as he said himself, "Introduced to the limitless, infinite and effulgent ocean of consciousness."

Ramakrishna adopted the art of renunciation and learned a non-dualist form of *Vedanta* philosophy from Totapuri. In this system, God is understood to be the formless, unmanifested energy that supports the cosmos. Ramakrishna experienced a deep form of trance (*nirvilkalpa samadhi*) under the guidance of his teacher. This state can be described as complete absorption of the soul into the divine ocean of consciousness. The new-found knowledge also contributed to his becoming 'Paramahamsa'.

❑

4

Amid the Sea of Meditation

"In the scriptures, you will find the way to realise God. But after getting all the information about the path to do so, you must begin to work towards the goal with all your might. Only then can you attain it. It's a tough call."

Bhairavi initiated Ramakrishna into the *tantrik* method of meditation. Initially, Ramakrishna was not comfortable with the idea of *tantrik* rituals, but once he dug deeper, he went on to master the art. He had already brought under his control the two roadblocks to attaining mastery in this method of meditation - attraction and aversion. Powers he acquired one too many, but as mentioned earlier, he was averse to using them. He could identify birds by their chirping, he could even understand their language. What is inaudible to the human ear was audible to Ramakrishna. Be that as it may, he never let a shred of arrogance take over his humility. His absolute faith in becoming one with God was based on the tripartite principle of devotion, knowledge and love.

From time immemorial, '*Om*' has been the primary source of strength in Hinduism. That it is the symbol representing the omnipotent, the omnipresent and is the source of all manifest existence was recognised by Ramakrishna. He acknowledged the symbol as being a bridge to the attempt to realise the Unknowable. *Om*, he emphasized, represents both the unmanifest (*nirguna*) and manifest (*saguna*) aspects of God. Even in our holy scriptures, it has been designated as *pranava*, to mean that it pervades life and runs through our life (*prana*). Even today, *Om* runs through our daily lives. We begin our prayers with the utterance, our rituals, our journeys, our everyday schedule – nothing is left untouched by its profundity. So much so, it is a popular symbol used in contemporary body art and tattoos.

Om runs through our daily lives. We begin our prayers with the utterance, our rituals, our journeys, our everyday schedule – nothing is left untouched by its profundity. So much so, it is a popular symbol used in contemporary body art and tattoos.

Cut to 1864. This is an incident Ramakrishna loved to relate. There once came along to Dakhineshwar a hermit, a wanderer by nature, who was a devotee of Ramlalla (Lord Rama as a child). Ramakrishna recollected, "The day I saw him, I knew he was no ordinary *sadhu*. His love for Ramlalla was unbound. He worshipped Ramlalla's idol each day and tend to him like a father. But there soon arose a problem. As days passed, Ramlalla grew more fond of me than him. I would see him wandering into the river, scold him that he would catch cold. He would make faces at me, run amok and do exactly the opposite of what I told him, the way any child would. I would at times lose my temper and yell at him. He would stop right in the tracks and give me a sullen look with tears in his eyes. My anger would obviously melt away. There was an instance he demanded I take him out for a swim. He was recalcitrant and my dissuasion made no difference. I had no option, but to let him accompany me. Once into the river, however, he began to sink and started gasping for breath. I had to literally carry him out of the water in my arms."

The bond between the two grew stronger. "Gradually," Ramakrishna said, "Ramlalla would walk into my room and insist he would stay there. When I would tell him that he should go back to the hermit's room because that's where he should be, he would refuse.

The bond between the two grew stronger. "Gradually," Ramakrishna said, "Ramlalla would walk into my room and insist he would stay there. When I would tell him that he should go back to the hermit's room because that's where he should be, he would refuse. One day, the hermit came to my room searching for him. 'You wouldn't care for your father, would you?' he thundered. 'I called out for you several times, but to no avail. I have cooked food for you, but you wouldn't even care to respond.' Having said this, he dragged a wailing Ramlalla to his own room. As evening descended, the hermit came back to my room. His anger had dissipated and there was calm writ large on his face. 'Ramlalla wants to stay here with you. I guess my happiness lies in fulfilling his wishes. I have nothing more to achieve. I have served my

> *One day, the hermit came to my room searching for him. 'You wouldn't care for your father, would you?' he thundered. 'I called out for you several times, but to no avail. I have cooked food for you, but you wouldn't even care to respond.'*

Lord and my senses have tasted sweet fulfillment in this pursuit. I guess it is time for me to leave.' The hermit was never to be seen again."

One of the oft-quoted statements of Ramakrishna is about God being the absolute truth. He said that unless one always speaks the truth, one cannot find God. It's only through truth that one can realise God. Ramakrishna believed that one of the cornerstones of truth is that all religions have the same purpose – help devotees find the route to be one with God.

From then on, Ramlalla's idol was kept in Dakhineshwar. It's unfortunately no longer there as it's rumoured to have been stolen. It remains traceless till date.

One of the oft-quoted statements of Ramakrishna is about God being the absolute truth. He said that unless one always speaks the truth, one cannot find God. It's only through truth that one can realise God. Ramakrishna believed that one of the cornerstones of truth is that all religions have the same purpose – help devotees find the route to be one with God. "I had to be one with all religions in order to be one with God," he used to say.

It was Ramakrishna's staunch belief that one must live by his own admission. To further his cause for monotheism, Ramakrishna embraced other religions like his own. When a *Sufi* saint by the name of Govind Ray came to Dakhineshwar, Ramakrishna was greatly impressed with his erudition and devotion. He started imbibing the doctrines of *Islam* from him. He even stopped going to the Kali temple and focused entirely on following the path of *Islam*. Three days after stern meditation, he became one with Prophet Mohammad who told him about 'one God', 'one religious journey' and how the myriad ways that different religions take converge at one point which we call God. "The ways are different, the aim is one," Ramakrishna had said.

On another occasion, Ramakrishna was standing outside a cathedral in Kolkata. He was taken in by the blessedness of the surroundings. Beaming at him was a painting of Mother Mary and Jesus Christ that embellished the wall of the church. He felt as if rays from the painting were piercing into his body. So moved was he by the milieu that he decided to follow the ways of Christianity for the next few days. Some three days later, he was taking a stroll at Panchwati when he suddenly saw a divine being clad in white walking towards him. "Who could he be?" Ramakrishna thought. "Jesus Christ," a voice from within said. They walked towards each other until Christ embraced Ramakrishna and became one with him. "Have any of you read the *Bible*?" Ramakrishna often asked his disciples. "How has Jesus Christ been described there? When I saw him, I found his nose slightly flattened. Is it true?" It was this childlike truthfulness that made Ramakrishna so endearing to his followers. He embodied all that was pure, untarnished and tactless – the hallmark of a Paramahamsa.

There is a place called Kolutola in Kolkata which has a Vaishnav temple. On one of his sojourns, Ramakrishna came across a huge gathering at the temple, all of whom were devotees of Chaitanya Mahaprabhu. There was an empty space where Mahaprabhu is believed to have sat. People were gathered around the space and singing *kirtans*. As the notes of the *kirtans* reached a crescendo,

Ramakrishna went into a trance and as if prod by an impulse, went over and sat on the empty space. A stunned silence followed. It was only natural that this touched a raw nerve with Mahaprabhu's devotees. They assembled at Bhagwandas Vaishnavi's place, who was the spiritual head of the Vaishnavis. Bhagwandas was not acquainted with Ramakrishna's stature. Aggrieved by such an act of temerity, he warned his disciples that similar acts should not be tolerated in the future.

Some time lapsed and Ramakrishna decided to visit Mahaprabhu's birthplace in Nadia district in Paschimbanga. Accompanied by Hriday, he stopped at Kalna *en route* to Nadia. Kalna, incidentally, happened to be the place where Bhagwandas resided. Both went to meet the seer. Hriday went inside the house first while Ramakrishna decided to wait. The moment Bhagwandas saw Hriday, he asked, "But you weren't supposed to come alone. A divine soul was supposed to accompany you." At this point, Ramakrishna entered the scene. A brief introduction followed following which Hriday queried, "You meditate and teach meditation as well. After reaching an exalted stage like yours, does one still need to meditate?" Bhagwandas replied, "I don't, but I do so only to inspire my disciples to reach the ultimate stage of meditation."

Bhagwandas' condescending tone upset Ramakrishna, who hadn't imagined a seer of his stature to have deep shades of pride in his demeanour. As was his wont, he lost his cool and snapped, "Who do you think you are? Do you think you are teaching them meditation? It's God who is providing all the strength to do so. You are nothing without him. Whoever made you a Guru?" He was so livid that he was literally shaking. Bhagwandas knew he was confronting no less than an incarnate. He realised his mistake. He knew that the man standing before him was the one who had sat on the sacred empty space of Mahaprabhu in Kolkata. He apologized to Ramakrishna and admitted, "Only you are the one who befits the holy seat of the Mahaprabhu."

Post Rani Rashmoni's demise, Mathur Babu's intimacy with Ramakrishna grew by leaps and bounds. Interestingly, he was initially suspicious of Ramakrishna's powers. The unimpeachable faith came after a string of incidents which convinced

"Can a plant have flowers of two different colours? Prove his prowess to me," Mathur Babu countered Ramakrishna. The following day while taking a stroll in the temple garden, Ramakrishna spotted a hibiscus plant with two flowers of different colours on the same branch, one red and the other white.

Mathur Babu of the seer's divinity and God-consciousness. There is an instance when Mathur Babu challenged Ramakrishna that even God cannot change the laws of nature. "Can a plant have flowers of two different colours? Prove his prowess to me," he countered Ramakrishna. The following day while taking a stroll in the temple garden, Ramakrishna spotted a hibiscus plant with two flowers of different colours on the same branch, one red and the other white. "See, God can do anything. Everything depends on His will," Ramakrishna said. Mathur Babu decided never to pose a challenge to Ramakrishna again.

As the bonding cemented further, Mathur Babu grew increasingly religious and began to frequently go on pilgrimage to Kashi, Mathura and Brindavan with his wife. It was January, 1868 that Mathur Babu requested Ramakrishna to accompany him on one of his pilgrimage. "Why not?" Ramakrishna was overwhelmed with joy. The first leg of the journey began and all set out on foot for Baidyanath Dham. On way, Ramakrishna was aghast to see the stinging poverty of the Adivasi tribals who had assembled on both sides of the road to see him. Ramakrishna sprang a surprise request on Mathur Babu. "You are Maa's child. Can you withstand the plight of your brothers? Provide food and *shawls* to these hapless people immediately." Mathur Babu was stunned. He mumbled an excuse that this pilgrimage would cost considerably and these people were too many in number. Ramakrishna lost his cool. "Get lost, you fool. I will not go with you. These people have no one to care for them. I will stay with them," he reprimanded Mathur Babu, cancelled his trip and stayed on with the tribals. Serving our fellowmen is true service to God. Ramakrishna lived by this principle, leading by example and inspiring people to do likewise.

Ramakrishna's going into a trance to be one with the Mother fascinated Mathur Babu to no end. He would often pester Ramakrishna 'Baba' to teach him how to go into a *samadhi*. By now, he knew that God resided in this empty shell we call the human body. "It's not something to be taught," Ramakrishna tried to reason. "It's something that happens by itself. You need to wait for the right time." Mathur Babu obstinately held on to his plea. "If you request Maa, She will acquiesce," Mathur Babu kept insisting. Ramakrishna finally gave in to his insistence. "So be it, I will request Maa. The rest is up to Her," he said.

Mathur Babu would often pester Ramakrishna 'Baba' to teach him how to go into a samadhi. By now, he knew that God resided in this empty shell we call the human body. "It's not something to be taught," Ramakrishna tried to reason. "It's something that happens by itself. You need to wait for the right time."

Some days later, on a trip to Kolkata, Mathur Babu went into a trance. It wasn't a complete *samadhi*, but he experienced shivers of a similar kind. "Mathur was a changed man hence," Ramakrishna recalled. "He became quiet, could not concentrate on anything and burst out crying on hearing Maa Kali's name." Meanwhile, Mathur Babu could not sleep for days. Restlessness had gripped him and he felt he was going mad. He rushed to Ramakrishna, fell at his feet and wailed, "Baba, enough of *samadhi*. I don't want any of it. I am going crazy. Please help me." Ramakrishna smiled, rubbed his chest and in some time, Mathur Babu came back to his normal state. The incident proved *samadhis* aren't easy, as isn't the road to be one with the Almighty.

Sixteen years of his association with Ramakrishna later, Mathur Babu fell ill with typhoid, then a dreadful ailment. Ramakrishna did not go to meet him, not once. He knew the end was near. His heart wrenched at the thought of Mathur Babu passing away. He sent Hriday instead to enquire about his health. One day, he forbade Hriday to visit Mathur Babu and went into a *samadhi*. Once back from the trance, said, "Mathur Babu has left us for the heavenly abode." Later that night, the news was confirmed.

It is said that when a disciple asked Ramakrishna if Mathur Babu may be born again, he quipped, "Well, he might come back as a prince this time."

❑

5

The Fragrance Spreads

"God is in all men, but all men are not in God. That is why we suffer."

It is said that the fragrance of flowers spreads only in the direction of the wind, but the goodness of a person spreads in all directions. Soon enough, Ramakrishna's name started making the rounds in almost every household in the entire state. This is the time when he came into contact with leading lights like Devendranath Thakur, Keshab Chandra Sen and Swami Dayanand. It would, however, be interesting to begin this chapter with an encounter Ramakrishna had with renowned scholar-reformist, Ishwar Chandra Vidyasagar.

At the time, Vidyasagar resided in Central Kolkata. His ancestral village Birsingha in Paschim Midnapore district of Paschimbanga was adjacent to Kamarpukur. Vidyasagar's life was devoted to the uplift of the downtrodden and the oppressed. His erudition apart, what made him stand out was his love for humanity and his unflinching zeal in supporting the cause of widow remarriage then considered a sacrilege. Vidyasagar did not believe that money was enough to ease the sufferings of humanity. He opened the doors of the Sanskrit College to lower caste students (previously it was exclusive to the Brahmins), nursed sick cholera patients, went to crematoriums to bury unclaimed dead bodies, dined with the untouchables and walked miles as a messenger-man to take urgent messages to people. Shortly after Vidyasagar's death, Rabindranath Tagore wrote about him: "One wonders how God, in the process of producing 40 million Bengalis, produced a man."

One day, Ramakrishna asked one of his disciples, Mahendranath to fix up a meeting with Vidyasagar. His curiosity was no less than that of Vidyasagar who had always wanted to meet the man they called 'Paramahamsa.' Vidyasagar often enquired of his acquaintances about Ramakrishna, if he looked like a typical sage, if he wore a *sadhu's* attire and such nitty-gritty. When told that Ramakrishna was a simple person like any other, his curiosity doubled. A meeting was fixed for a particular Saturday.

Ramakrishna arrived at the palatial building where Vidyasagar lived which had all the stately trappings of the British Raj. Vidyasagar rose to welcome Ramakrishna. A mammoth of humanity gathered to watch how the two towering personalities interacted. Taking a cue from his name Vidyasagar (ocean of knowledge), Ramakrishna said, "I have hitherto gone to streams and lakes and rivers. This is my first brush with an ocean." "Well," smiled Vidyasagar, "I guess you will only take back salty water from this ocean." "Not in the least. You are indeed an ocean of knowledge," said Ramakrishna. The gathering burst out laughing, the ice was broken and the stage set for a more staid discourse.

For hours together, the two discussed various subjects. From the world of duality and transcendental nature of Brahmin, citing the parables of the salt doll, the woodcutter and the ant and the sugar hill, on discrimination between true and false knowledge, on different manifestations of God's power, on ego and suffering and on the power of faith. Vidyasagar was moved by such depth of thought from a person whose formal education was but perfunctory. As the topic veered to faith and God, Ramakrishna said, "God cannot be known by bookish knowledge, howsoever deep. One needs to feel him in his own being. I will relate an incident. Once on a pilgrimage, Chaitanyadev saw a man reading the *Bhagavad Gita* and weeping. Chaitanyadev was moved by the sight. He approached the man and asked him if he understood what was written in the *Gita*. The man replied he did not understand a word of what was written and he didn't know Sanskrit either. But as he read the holy scriptures, he could see before him Lord Krishna and Arjuna with the former explaining certain things which he could not understand. Yet, the very scene moved him to tears. That's how you can know God. No argument can suffice. The root of our sufferings is that we have become so self-centric that we can't look beyond ourselves. Realise Him to know Him. Else, you move further away."

The more Ramakrishna spoke, the more it fascinated Vidyasagar. He had never known logic to be so lucid, never had he known that the concept of God-consciousness could be so trenchantly elucidated. The parting words of Ramakrishna stuck to him for long, "The only way to know God is *Samadhi*, surrender and love."

Among those who were influenced by Ramakrishna were Kehshab Chandra Sen and Devendranath Tagore. Both were associated with the Brahmo Samaj, the societal component of the Brahmo religion. It was one of the most influential religious movements responsible for the making of modern India. It was conceived in Kolkata in 1830 by Devendranath Tagore and Ram Mohan Roy as reformation of the prevailing Brahminism of the time and began the Bengal Renaissance of the 19th century pioneering all religious, social and educational advance of the Hindu community.

Devendranath Tagore was a Hindu philosopher and religious reformer. He was one of the founders of the Brahmo religion. He was a deeply religious man. In 1848, Devendranath codified the Adi Dharma doctrine as Brahmo Dharma Beej (Seed of the Brahmo Dharma). In 1850, he published a book titled *'Brahmo Dharma'* enshrining the principles emphasizing monotheism, rationality and mediation between man and God.

Like Devendranath, Keshab Chandra Sen too was a Hindu philosopher and social reformer who attempted to incorporate the Christian theology within the framework of Hindu thought. He became a member of the Brahmo Samaj in 1856, but founded his own breakaway 'Brahmo Samaj of India' in 1866, while the Brahmo Samaj remained under the leadership of Devendranath. Later in his life, he came under the influence of Ramakrishna and founded a syncretic '*Nobobidhan*' or 'New Dispensation' inspired by Christianity, *Vaishnav bhakti* and Hindu practices.

Sen was won over to Ramakrishna less by his teachings and more by his unconventional, eccentric manners. When Ramakrishna met him, he had accepted Christianity and had separated from the Brahmo Samaj. Formerly, Sen had rejected idolatry practised by his family, but after coming under Ramakrishna's influence, again accepted Hindu polytheism and established the 'New Dispensation' religious movement, which was based on Ramakrishna's principles — 'Worship of God as Mother' and 'All religions as true.' His acceptance of idolatry also created factions within his Samaj. Sen publicised Ramakrishna's teachings in the journals of 'New Dispensation' over several years, which led to Ramakrishna gaining popularity among a wider audience, especially the *Bhadralok* and Europeans residing in India.

Sen got his daughter married off at the age of 14 to the Maharaja of Cooch Behar. This, being in contravention to the rules of the Brahmo Samaj, was vehemently opposed by the members. He was castigated and vilified. Sen was deeply hurt. The man to stand beside him at the hour of distress was Ramakrishna who taught him to cope with adversity. So fond did Ramakrishna become of Sen that after the latter's demise, he said, "I am shattered. Half of me has perished."

Talking of Sen's initial cynicism regarding Ramakrishna, here's an interesting bit. When they first met in 1876, Ramakrishna's rough and unsophisticated exterior repelled Sen and he showed no affinity towards the former's mysticism. Ramakrishna's trance did not impress him either. It was only after a detailed discourse that Sen gradually began realising Ramakrishna's potential. "Four blind men who were travelling together met an elephant on the way," Ramakrishna said. "The first touched the elephant's ears and opined the tusker was like a *soop* (a gadget used for winnowing of grain). The second touched its feet and said the elephant was more like a tree. All four touched different parts of the elephant and gave their own opinion. God's like that. Everyman has his own opinion. And that's the absolute truth for him."

Ramakrishna went on to give another instance. A man was standing near a tree when he saw a chameleon. He said it was red in colour. Another man standing nearby contradicted him and said it was green. A third swore it was blue. The skirmish among the three attracted the attention of a fourth who came in to mediate. He pacified the people and told them that they were all correct in their own ways. The chameleon could change its colour of its own volition. "This is the will of God that He has given such power to the chameleon. This proves His existence," the mediator reasoned.

Ramakrishna's anecdotes were so down-to-earth, so real that one could live them. This pragmatism acquired by experience made a dent on Sen's mind. Before leaving, Ramakrishna's guffawed, "Keshab, your tail has fallen off." A puzzled Sen looked for answers. Ramakrishna explained thus, "When a tadpole is born, it has a tail so that it can swim in water. As time passes by, its tail falls off. Then it is ready to swim in water just as easily as it can tread on the ground. Likewise, once the tail of ignorance forsakes a man, he can strike a balance between both the material and divine worlds with equal ease. You are now ready to straddle both worlds. Remember, love God like your father. Don't ask questions. A child doesn't ask his father any questions. He simply obeys his orders and the rest is up to the father to look after the child."

Another prominent figure who brushed shoulders with Ramakrishna during that period was Pandit Bijoy Krishna Goswami, a prominent social reformer and religious figure. He was a spokesman of the new Vaisnavite doctrine. Inspired by Devendranath Tagore, he joined Brahmo Samaj. In his lifetime Bijoy Krishna visited various states to preach Brahmonism. Later, he decided to traverse different religious paths to attain the absolute truth. Even in doing so, he was unable to find it. He then understood the importance of a Guru. He became a disciple of Brahmananda Paramahamsa and worked his way to the absolute truth, which he then preached to many. His teachings are documented in the book '*Sri Sri Sadgurusanga.*' His rapport with Ramakrishna brought him closer to love, surrender and sacrifice. Even after becoming a spiritual leader in his own right, Goswami never fought shy of admitting his indebtedness to Ramakrishna. So did Trilokyanath Sanyal, composer with the Samaj, whose association with Ramakrishna gave Bengal several devotional tunes which he called Bramha Sangeet which, till date, remain popular in the state.

As time passed, Ramakrishna became more popular. His followers were increasing. Not because he was supremely erudite, but perhaps because of the lack of it. Suddenly, the people found all hocus-pocus and tall talks involved in religious discourses gone. Here was a man – filled with divine power yet egoless and humble – of unsurpassed knowledge. Here was someone quite unlettered, yet married with an extended family of mind-born children, down-to-earth and practical. Simple and unostentatious, devoid of material wealth, possessed of an encyclopedic knowledge of the ancient scriptures and an uncanny ability to fathom the depths of the human mind, Ramakrishna would preach the *Vedanta* to everyone, both scholarly and unlettered. He would encourage, rather than discourage people. If someone asked, "Baba, I am a sinner. How can I make amends?" he would give a smile of benediction and say, "If you think you are a sinner, you become one. If you have God's name on your lips, how can you possibly be a sinner? It's Him first and then the worldly matters. Believe in Him." It's this "belief" that bound the endless stream of devotees who now frequented Dakhineshwar to have a glimpse of the man who never attempted to form a religion or an institution. He didn't need to. He had become an institution unto himself.

❑

6

Vivekananda is Born

"If you desire to be pure, have firm faith and slowly proceed with your devotional practices without wasting your energy in useless scriptural discussions and arguments. Your little brain will otherwise be muddled."

Ramakrishna often told his disciples about a vision he had during one of his *samadhis*. "Ifound my mind soaring high along a luminous path. As it went higher, I found on both sides of the way ideal forms of Gods and Goddesses. As the mind reached the outer limits of the region, the mind entered the transcendental realm where no corporal being was visible. But the next moment I saw several sages seated there in *Samadhi*. It struck me that the sages must have surpassed not only men but even Gods in knowledge and holiness, in renunciation and love. I was lost in admiration when I suddenly saw a portion of the undifferentiated luminous region condense into the form of a divine child. The child approached a sage, addressed him in a sweet chirpy voice and tried to drag him out of his *samadhi*. The child's touch roused the sage, while the child spoke, "I am going down. You must come with me." "The sage remained mute, but his tender look expressed assent."

Ramakrishna said that the day he saw Vivekananda, he knew him to be the sage he saw during his *samadhi*. It was much later that he disclosed that the divine child was none other than himself.

Vivekananda was born as Narendranath Dutta in Kolkata (then Calcutta) on January 12, 1863. After years of practiced austerity and obeisance to Lord Shiva in Varanasi, Narendra was born to Bhuvaneshwari Devi, a deeply religious woman who instilled traditional values in her children. "Remain pure, guard your honour and never vitiate the honour of your fellow beings. Balance tranquillity of the heart with hardened stance, whenever necessary." Narendra's father, Vishwanath Dutta, an attorney with the Calcutta High Court, was a compassionate gentleman with a progressive mindset.

Brought up in this milieu of the best of both traditional and modern, Narendra grew up to be quite a precocious child. This was 19th Century Calcutta and Bengal was transforming in the midst of Renaissance. From an early age, Narendra was taught to live by one principle - not to accept anything without evidence. He had a photographic memory and could remember anything he read once with clinical precision. Despite his brilliant academic performance in subjects like history, philosophy and literature, he staunchly held on to his conviction not to believe what one read in a book. He realised that the essence of life lay in finding out the truth for oneself. Ramakrishna once said of him: "Narendra is a great soul - unimpeachable in meditation. He cuts the veils of *maya* to pieces with the rapier of knowledge. He can never be enticed by *maya*." Once a cobra appeared when Narendra was meditating with his friends. The other boys were frightened and ran away. But Narendra remained motionless. The cobra, after lingering for a while, crawled away. Later, Narendra told his parents: "I knew nothing of the snake. I was lost in meditation and was experiencing ineffable joy."

At the age of fifteen he experienced spiritual ecstasy. He was journeying with his family to Raipur in Central India, and part of the trip had to be made in a bullock-cart. It was a beautiful day and the cart was moving through a narrow pass where the lofty peaks rising on both sides almost touched each other. Narendra caught sight of a large beehive in the cleft of a giant cliff. The hive must have been there a very long time. Suddenly, his mind was filled with awe and reverence for the Divine Providence, and he lost outer consciousness. Perhaps this was the first time that his powerful imagination helped him to ascend to the realm of the superconscious.

As a student, Narendra had a vision which he related thus: "One night I was meditating behind closed doors and had a fairly deep concentration of mind. How long I meditated I cannot say. After the meditation was over, I remained seated. Then from the southern wall of that room a luminous figure stepped out and stood in front of me. It was the figure of a *sannyasi* (monk), absolutely calm, with shaven head, and staff and *kamandalu* (water pot) in either hand. He gazed at me for some time, and seemed as if he would address me. I, too, gazed at him in speechless wonder. Suddenly a kind of fright seized me. I opened the door and hurried out of the room. Then it struck me that it was foolish of me to run away like that. Perhaps, he might have said something to me. But I have never seen that figure since. I think it was the Lord Buddha whom I saw."

Principal William Hastie of General Assembly's Institution (now Scottish Church College), is said to have observed: "Narendranath is really a genius. I have travelled far and wide, but I have never yet come across a lad of his talents and possibilities, even in German universities, amongst philosophical students."

Brajendra Nath Seal, Narendra's fellow student, who later became a leading Indian philosopher, wrote in his memoirs: "Narendra was a gifted youth, sociable, free and unconventional in manners, a sweet singer, the soul of social circles, a brilliant conversationalist, at times bitter and caustic, piercing with the shafts of keen witticism the shows and mummeries of the world, sitting in the scorner's chair but hiding the most tender of hearts under that garb of cynicism. He was an inspired bohemian, but possessed what bohemians lack - an iron will; somewhat peremptory and absolute, speaking with accents of authority and withal possessing a strange power of the eye which could hold his listeners in thrall."

A genius from a young age, Narendra had a volley of talent - he was a musician, debater, gymnast, philanthropist, an ideal yogi, mystic, ascetic, worker, and philosopher. He was energy personified. He once told a disciple: "In my childhood, I used to feel an inexhaustible force arising in me, overflowing in my body. I used to become restless and could not keep quiet. This was why I used to fidget all the time... My insides would vibrate, as it were, and make me restless." Romain Rolland, the famed French writer and Swami Vivekananda's biographer, wrote: "He was athletic, tall and trained to excel in all kinds of sports. He had an olive complexion, a full face, vast forehead, strong jaw, a pair of magnificent eyes, large, dark and rather prominent, with heavy lids, whose shape recalled the classic comparison to a lotus petal. Nothing escaped the magic of his glance, capable equally of embracing in its irresistible charm, or of sparkling with wit, irony, or kindness, of losing itself in ecstasy, of plunging imperiously to the very depths of consciousness and of withering with its fury. But his pre-eminent characteristic was kingliness. He was a born king and nobody ever came near him either in India or America without paying homage to his majesty."

In his intense desire to realise the truth, young Narendra practised meditation, studied different religious and philosophical systems of the East and the West, met different religious leaders, but nothing seemed to bear fruit. He even joined the Brahmo Samaj, a socio-religious organisation, and asked its leader, Devendranath Tagore, "Sir, have you seen God?" Devendranath was embarrassed and replied: "My boy, you have the eyes of a yogi. You should practise meditation."

Then came the turning point in his life. His first introduction to Ramakrishna occurred one day during a literature class, when he heard Professor W.W. Hastie lecturing on English poet, William Wordsworth's 'The Excursion' and the poet's mysticism involving nature. Hastie told his students that with purity and concentration such transcendental experience was possible, but in modern times it had become extremely rare. "I have known only one person," he said, "Who has realised that blessed state and he is Ramakrishna of Dakhineshwar. You will understand this concept better if you visit this saint." Narendra knew where his next stop would be.

The first meeting was destined to happen in Calcutta in November, 1881 at the house of Ramakrishna's devotee, Surendra Nath Mitra. Surendra had arranged a religious gathering and had invited Narendra to entertain Ramakrishna and the gathering with his devotional songs. A few minutes after Narendra started singing,

Ramakrishna went into a trance. A stunned silence followed and Narendra was taken aback by the sudden development. Ramakrishna soon came back to his normal self and requested Narendra to continue singing. Once the singing was over, Ramakrishna dragged Narendra to one corner and said, "You must come to Dakhineshwar. I will be waiting for you. Do come soon."

This was the time when Narendra, who was 18, was being coaxed by his father to get married. There was a proposal where the girl's father tried to trade his daughter who was dark-complexioned for a huge sum of money as dowry. Narendra flatly refused. His cousin Ramchandra Dutta was given the responsibility to make him agree to the wedlock. Soon enough, Ramchandra realised that it was beyond his capacity to make Narendra fall in line. It was he who suggested it was time for him to visit Ramakrishna in Dakhineshwar.

Narendra first visited Dakhineshwar sometime in the early part of 1882. He entered Ramakrishna's room through the western door that faces the *Ganges*. Indifferent to his external appearance, Narendra's clothes were dishevelled; his impressive eyes were partly indrawn. Ramakrishna marvelled: "How is it that such a great spiritual aspirant can live in Calcutta, the home of the worldly-minded?" He took Narendra to the temple. There was a mat spread out on the floor. Ramakrishna asked him to sit and requested him to sing a song. Narendra sang a song of the Brahmo Samaj, which if translated, would go something like this:

"Let us go back once more,
O mind, to our proper home,
Here in this foreign land of earth
Why should we wander aimlessly in a
stranger's guise?..."

This song transported Ramakrishna into a state of ecstasy. When the singing was over, he took Narendra to the northern verandah of the temple and closed the door. With tearful eyes, he said to Narendra: "You have come so late. Was that proper? Couldn't you have guessed how I have been waiting for you? My ears are nearly burned off, listening to the talk of these worldly people. I thought I should burst, not having anyone to tell how I really felt."

Then with folded hands, he continued: "I know who you are, my Lord. You are Nara, the ancient sage, the incarnation of Narayana. You have come to earth to take away the sufferings and sorrows of mankind." The rationality in Narendra was shaken. He stood transfixed, regarding this as the babble of an insane person. "I am Vishwanath Dutta's son. I have never known or seen him. How is it that he claims to have known me for a long time and had been waiting for me?"

When they returned to Ramakrishna's room, Narendra's mind was agitated by Ramakrishna's peculiar conduct. However, he asked what he often asked all religious people, "Sir, have you seen God?" Without a moment's hesitation, Ramakrishna replied: "Yes indeed, I have seen Him. I see Him as I see you here, only more clearly. God can be seen. One can talk to Him. But who cares for God? People shed torrents of tears for their wives, children, wealth, and property, but who weeps for the vision of God? If one cries sincerely for God, one can surely see Him."

"That impressed me at once," Narendra later told his disciples. "For the first time, I found a man who dared to say that he had seen God, that religion was a reality to be felt, to be sensed in an infinitely more intense way than we can sense the world." Narendra felt that Ramakrishna's words were uttered from the depths of his inner experience. Still, he could not comprehend the true meaning of the words. Bewildered, he returned to Kolkata.

The abruptness in Ramakrishna's demeanour left Narendra shocked. "Is he mad?" said his conscious mind. He tried to forget the matter as a coincidence. His subconscious, however, kept nudging him. "Aren't we all mad in some way or the other? Every great man has a streak of madness about him. Maybe, you should probe further and visit him again in Dakhineshwar."

After a month's procrastination, Narendra returned to Dakhineshwar. He found Ramakrishna alone in his room. Ramakrishna was glad to see Narendra and asked him to sit on the corner of his bed. After a few minutes, Ramakrishna came closer in an ecstatic mood, muttered some words, fixed his eyes on him and placed his right foot on Narendra's body. At his touch, Narendra saw, with open eyes, the whole world vanishing - the walls, the room, the temple garden and even himself had disappeared into the void. He was sure he was facing death. He cried out loudly: "What on earth are you doing to me? Don't you know that I have parents back at home?"

Ramakrishna burst out laughing, gently touched Narendra's chest and said: "All right, let it stop now. It will happen in its own good time." With this, Narendra became normal again.

Normal wouldn't be the right word though. Narendra might have felt better, but his mind was warped with thoughts of the rather mysterious happening. He was a changed person. He simply failed to comprehend what had happened. Narendra was proud of his strong body, mind and rational intellect. But he felt helpless in front of Ramakrishna as he could not control himself. During his third visit to Dakhineshwar, he tried his utmost to be on guard. Ramakrishna took him out for a walk to Jadu Mallik's garden house where they both sat down in the parlour. Then Ramakrishna went into an ecstatic mood and touched Narendra, who lost outer consciousness. In that state, Ramakrishna asked Narendra questions about his past, his mission in the world, the duration of his present life and so on. The answers only confirmed what he had seen about Narendra in the vision he had experienced many years before.

Later, Ramakrishna told his disciples: "Narendra is a great soul, perfect in meditation. The day he recognises his true self, he will give up his body by an act of will through yoga."

The meeting of Narendra and Ramakrishna was an important event. It was like a meeting between the occident and the orient, the modern and the ancient. Ramakrishna tamed the rebellious Narendra with his infinite patience, love, and vigilance. He was convinced of Narendra's divine nature and mission to the world.

Despite Narendra's best attempts, he could not keep his mind off Ramakrishna. He kept visiting Dakhineshwar for six years hence. He was in no hurry to become Ramakrishna's disciple. He wasn't still certain of Ramakrishna's powers. Ramakrishna would nevertheless support Narendra to the hilt. "It's fine if you do not believe me. Why should you take my words for granted. Let the mind be free of cobwebs. Your heart will tell you when to believe me," Ramakrishna told Narendra.

In the early part of 1884, Narendra's father died unexpectedly of a heart attack. Unfortunately, he left behind many unsettled debts and the once well-to-do family was suddenly thrust into acute poverty. To add to their troubles, some relatives filed a lawsuit with the intent of depriving them of their home. Since Narendra was the eldest son, the responsibility for the family's welfare fell upon his shoulders. He had just passed his B.A. examination and had been admitted to law school. On many occasions, he would attend his classes without having eaten and would faint due to hunger and weakness. He had no job and, moreover, no previous work experience.

Forced by circumstances, Narendra began visiting business and government offices for a job. Occasionally, one of his friends, who knew the gravity of his situation, anonymously sent modest amounts of money to Narendra's mother. His friends invited him now and then to their homes and offered him food, but the thought of his hungry mother, sisters, and brothers at home prevented him from eating. At home he would eat as little as possible in order that the others might have enough. This first contact with the harshness of life convinced Narendra that unselfish sympathy is rare in this world. There is no place here for the weak, the poor and the destitute. The realization itself was the first step Narendra took towards the attainment of the absolute truth.

Narendra later related how the world tries to take advantage of a person's miseries. "Various temptations came my way. A rich woman sent me an ugly proposal to end my days of penury, which I sternly rejected. Another woman also made similar overtures. I said to her: 'You have wasted your life seeking the pleasures of the flesh. The dark shadows of death are before you. Have you done anything to face that? Give up all these filthy desires and remember God."

One day, after a futile search for a job, Narendra was sitting at a park. A friend who happened to be with him wanted to console him with a song: "Here blows the wind, the breath of Brahman; It is His grace we feel." Narendra furiously blurted out: "Be quiet! That fanciful nonsense is apt for people living in the lap of luxury - people who have no idea what hunger is. It sounds true and beautiful to them - as it did to me. But now I have seen what life is really like. That song is just a pack of lies."

Despite what he said to his friend, Narendra did not lose his inherent faith in God and His mercy. He used to repeat the Lord's name as he got out of bed in the morning. One day his mother overheard him and said bitterly: "Shut up, you fool! You have been crying yourself hoarse for God since your childhood. Tell me what has God done for you?" These words stung Narendra to an extent that it turned him into an atheist. Doubts clouded his mind about God's existence and His providence. It was not in his nature to hide his feelings. He began to tell people aggressively that God did not exist and that praying to him was also futile. The rumour soon spread that Narendra had become an atheist.

As the word spread like wildfire, it reached Ramakrishna's ears. He, however, paid no attention. When a friend of Narendra tearfully told Ramakrishna, "Sir, we never imagined Narendra would sink so low," the latter shot back, "Silence, you scoundrels! Maa Kali has told me that it is simply not true."

Narendra, meanwhile, knew it was the end of the road to worldly matters for him. He secretly prepared to renounce the world. When he heard that Ramakrishna was visiting a devotee in Kolkata, he decided to see him before he left his home forever. When they met, Ramakrishna persuaded Narendra to accompany him to Dakhineshwar. When they arrived in his room, Ramakrishna went into an ecstasy and sang a song, which clearly indicated that he knew Narendra's secret plan. That night he sent the others away and said to Narendra with tears: "I know you have come to the world to do Mother's work and you can never lead a worldly life. But, for my sake, stay with your family as long as I am alive."

Narendra agreed. The next day he returned home and managed to find a temporary job in an attorney's office, which was sufficient to cover the bare expenses of his family. But he couldn't bear that he couldn't do enough for his family. Suddenly, it struck him. Why not ask the Mother to ease his financial problems? He requested Ramakrishna to make the plea on his behalf. "Go to the Mother and ask Her yourself," Ramakrishna told him. Narendra went to the temple with great anticipation, but as soon as he came before the image of the Divine Mother, he saw Her as living and conscious. He forgot the world and the pitiable condition of his family. In ecstatic joy, he prostrated before Her and prayed: "Mother, give me discrimination! Give me renunciation! Give me knowledge and devotion! Grant that I may have an uninterrupted vision of Thee!"

He went back to the Master and told him what had happened. The Master sent Narendra to the temple to pray again, but the same thing happened. The third time he did remember his intention, but felt ashamed to ask for something so small from the Almighty for his own benefit. "I can't do it. You must help me," he surrendered to Ramakrishna. To this, Ramakrishna smiled and said, "All right, your people at home will never be in want of plain food and clothing."

Ramakrishna knew Narendra was finally ready to take the next big step forward. That day, Swami Vivekananda was born.

❑

7

The Trusted Apostles

"God can be realised through various paths. All religions are true. The important thing is to reach the roof. You can reach it using stone or wooden stairs, or a scaffolding, or even with the help of a rope. You can also climb up a pole and reach out to Him. Not the means, but the end is important."

Ramakrishna knew he wouldn't live long. He had a mission to accomplish. Perhaps he knew where the world was headed with changing times. He knew he couldn't propagate his messages of peace and religious amity without trusted lieutenants. Though Vivekananda was the first among his generals, there were others too. He had christened all his disciples. Some of them need special mention: Narendranath Dutt (Vivekananda), Rakhal Chandra Ghosh (Brahmananda), Latu (Adbhutananda), Gopal Ghosh (Advaitananda), Baburam Ghosh (Premananda), Nitya Ranjan Ghosh (Niranjanananda), Yogendranath Chaudhury (Yogananda), Sharatchandra Chakraborty (Shardananda), Shashibhushan Chakraborty (Ramkrishnananda), Taraknath Ghoshal (Shivananda), Harinath Chaterjee (Turiyananda), Subodhchandra Ghosh (Subodhananda), Gangadhar Ghatak (Akhandananda) and Kali Prasad Chandra (Abhedananda).

Given below are brief sketches of some of Ramakrishna's apostles. Without them, perhaps, Ramakrishna's mission would have remained half-accomplished.

Baburam Ghosh (Premananda) hailed from Hoogly's Anantpur village. Born in 1861, he was principal of a secondary school before he came into contact with Ramakrishna in 1882.

Affable and accessible, Ramakrishna said of him, "Baburam is an utensil in which milk never rots." Baburam was in charge of Belur Math from 1902 to 1916.

Nitya Ranjan Ghosh (Niranjanananda) was barely 18 when he met Ramakrishna. He had what people called *'divya drishti'* (divine insight) and would often be used as a medium for treatment of the ailing. Ramakrishna disliked the idea. He told Ghosh that he shouldn't fritter away his powers thus and should use it to concentrate and be one with God.

Ghosh was a good-hearted lad. The only drawback in his character was his awful temper. A warning came from Ramakrishna, "Anger is the greatest sin. If anyone abuses you, why do you need to react? Don't and the other person will gradually calm down."

Yogendranath Chaudhury (Yogananda) was 20 when Ramakrishna took him under his wings.

Yogendra was as inquisitive as Narendra. One night, when he did not see Ramakrishna in bed, he suspected him to have gone to Maa Sharda's room. Suspecting his master's intentions, he slowly crept out and hid behind a pillar to keep an eye on Maa Sharda's room. Ramakrishna who had gone elsewhere, suddenly emerged from behind and said in an appreciative tone (as appreciatively as he had once told Narendra), "Bravo, my boy. Before accepting anyone as your Guru, you must keep tab on his actions to examine his genuineness."

Ramakrishna called six of his disciples *'Eeshwarkoti'* (of the stature of the Almighty) and they included Narendra, Rakhal, Baburam, Niranjan, Yogendranath and **Purnachand Ghosh**. The last person mentioned, **Purnachand**, was only 13 when he came to Dakhineshwar. The moment Ramakrishna saw him, he asked, "My son, what do you think of me?" "I think, Sir," the teenager replied, "You are an incarnation of the Almighty whose has come in human form for the benefit of mankind." The maturity in his expression convinced Ramakrishna that Purnachand was no ordinary child.

Sharatchandra Chakraborty (Sharadananda) was 18 when he met Ramakrishna in 1883. His father wanted him to be a doctor and got him admitted to a medical college. But when Ramakrishna fell critically ill, he left college and became a *sannyasi*. He, however, never gave up treating the poor until his last breath. He met Vivekananda in London 1896. Vivekananda asked him to help him out in completing his mission and they collaborated during a tour to the US. He was designated the first secretary of the Ramakrishna Math and Mission.

Sashibhushan Chakraborty (Ramkrishnananda) set up the Ramakrishna Mission in Madras in 1897 and remained in charge of the same till his demise in 1911. He had forsaken his academic pursuit at the instance of Ramakrishna. He used to tell the young recruits at Ramakrishna Mission, "I teach because I consider it my duty. It's my prayer to God. Now whether you pay attention to my discourses is a matter of your conscience." He was, nonetheless, a strict disciplinarian within the precincts of the Mission. "No reading newspapers here, please," he used to tell devotees, "This is a place exclusively for offering prayers to the Almighty."

Taraknath Ghoshal (Shivananda) was 26 when he became Ramakrishna's disciple. That was 1880. His father was the legal consultant of Rani Rashmoni. Eminently amiable and blessed with a cheerful disposition, he was immensely popular among the devotees.

Harinath Chaterjee (Turiyananda) came from a conservative Brahmin family. Deeply religious, he meditated the whole night long which soon became second nature to him. Hardly was there any religious book which he hadn't read. At the age of 14, he met Ramakrishna. After becoming a *sannyasi*, he had a dream which inspired him to devote his life to the pursuit of the absolute truth.

He accompanied Vivekananda on his second trip to the US and was instrumental in setting up Ramakrishna Ashrams in cities like California and San Francisco. He believed in less words and more action as he firmly believed the latter had more steam. He spent most of his time in the US looking after the Ashrams. By the time he returned to India, Vivekananda had passed away.

Sharad Prasanna Mitra (Trigunatritananda) was a brilliant student and studied in the same school as Rakhal and Baburam. His despondency at having failed to make it at the Calcutta University entrance examinations drove him to Ramakrishna.

Later, he was sent to San Francisco to look after the Mission there. He set up the first Hindu Mandir (temple) in the US.

Subodhchandra Ghosh (Subodhananda) was born to parents who were devotees of Ramakrishna. His interest arose in Ramakrishna after reading a book gifted by his father.

The first time Subodh met Ramakrishna, the latter took his hand and said, "Maa has told me that you will accomplish your aim." Subodh was forthright and never shied away from calling a spade a spade. Not even if the person in question was his Master. Once when Ramakrishna asked him what he thought of his Master, he said without batting an eyelid, "Well, people say a lot of things about your capabilities. Due to lack of proof, I cannot prove them either right or wrong."

The man Vivekananda called *'khoka'* (meaning kid, as he was the youngest among the disciples), once fell severely ill in Rishikesh. Ramakrishna who paid him a visit, asked, "Should I send in a rich man who would take care of you in a more proper manner?" "No way," Subodh said, "I would like to remain ill, because then you are going to visit me more frequently."

Gadadhar Ghatak (Akhandananda) was brought to Dakhineshwar by Turiyananda. He remained close to Vivekananda till the very end. His service to mankind by way of spreading the light of education among the downtrodden and caring for the ailing, is still remembered today.

Hariprasanna Chaterjee (Vigyanananda) met Ramakrishna in strange circumstances. He was 18 and had gone to Dakhineshwar with his parents from Kolkata where he lived. He had heard a lot about Ramakrishna. He went to meet him. Devotees streamed to meet him in his room. One after another, they touched his feet and left. All at once, Hariprasanna realised he was all alone with Ramakrishna in the room. Ramakrishna gave him a piercing look and asked, "Want to wrestle with me?" A stout guy, Hariprasanna agreed. In no time, he had Ramakrishna pinned to the wall. Then, something strange happened. A flash of current seemed to pass through Hariprasanna and he went into a trance. When he came back to his senses, Ramakrishna smiled, "You have won. Keep coming to Dakhineshwar."

Having acquired a degree in civil engineering from Pune, Hariprasanna had a dream about Ramakrishna's demise. Later, he joined hands with Vivekananda to build Belur Math.

Kali Prasad Chandra (Abhedananda), a known Sanskrit scholar, was told by Ramakrishna that he was a yogi in his previous birth and this would be his last birth. Kali Prasad served Ramakrishna to the hilt when the latter fell terminally ill. He joined Vivekananda in London in 1896 and was put in charge of the Vedanta Samaj in 1897.

❑

8

Belief and Faith

"If you first fortify yourself with the true knowledge of the Universal Self and then live in the midst of wealth and worldliness, surely they will in no way affect you."

There is an interesting incident that happened in Germany. Vivekananda, who there on a visit, was the guest of celebrated German Orientalist and Sanskrit scholar, Professor Paul Deussen. One day, he saw Deussen in a pensive mood. "What's the matter?" asked Vivekananda. "I have been reading this book for 15 days, but have not been able to complete it. Worse, I can't understand what it's trying to say," said a disgusted Deussen. Vivekananda asked for the book. "What? But you don't know the German language," Deussen said in a perplexed tone. Vivekananda stood his ground, completed reading the book in one hour flat and answered all the queries of a stunned Deussen.

This supreme concentration is what, as Ramakrishna always said, meditation can achieve.

Ramakrishna's discussion always converged at one point - belief. He said that the roadblock to implicit belief is man's penchant for the dual culprits, 'Me' and 'Myself.' Half-baked belief can mar rather than make. Ramakrishna gave an example. Once, a man wanted to cross the sea from ancient Lanka. Ravana's brother Bivishana gave him a small packet, asked him to tie it to one end of his shirt and fly above the sea, warning him that he should never dare to open the packet. The man did as told and glided over the sea. Half way through, though, his belief gave way to suspicion. "What is it in the packet that's so powerful?" he thought. He opened the packet and saw the words 'Sree Ram' scribbled on a piece of paper. No sooner had he done that, than he fell into the sea. Lack of belief led him to his doom.

Speaking of belief, Mahendranath Gupta, who wrote '*Ramakrishna Kathamrita*' (Ramakrishna's messages) in the Bangla language, met Ramakrishna for the first time as a kid when he was lost in the mammoth crowd within the temple premises sometime in 1854. A divine figure appeared from nowhere, comforted the wailing child and reunited him with his mother. Mahendranath later realised that the divine figure was Ramakrishna.

Years passed by. Mahendranath came to Dakhineshwar to meet Ramakrishna one morning. The conversation that ensued went something like this:

Where do you live?

In Kolkata.

Where?

At Ishaan Kaviraj's house with my sister.

"Oh, then you know about Keshab (Chandra Sen). He was very sick. I had prayed to Maa Kali to cure him. If he doesn't live, who else will I have left in Calcutta? Have you heard of Cook Sahib? It was Keshab who took me to him. By the way, do you believe in *saakar* (form) or *nirakar* (formless) way of worshipping God?"

One can't believe in both all at once. One can believe in only one at a time. How can the colour of milk be white and black at the same time? As for me, I believe in *nirakar* worship.

It's good that one follows only one way of worship. But it's a matter of faith. How can you say that what you believe is right and the others aren't?

(*The import of Ramakrishna's words didn't register on Mahendranath's mind. He kept arguing*).

Even if we agree on giving a form to God, we can't say God resembles the earthen idols that artisans make?

Why do you go by the form the artist has given the idols? He has made them from his heart. The craftsmanship has emerged from the depths of his soul. Why do you Calcuttans always want to make people understand? The mother of

all questions is: have you understood yourself? Have you had self-realisation? Are you devoted enough for complete surrender? If you have understood God, why then try and make others understand?

(*Ramakrishna's utterances were gradually digging into Mahendranath. Reams and reams of passages from books do not help you 'feel' God. Your 'inner eye' does. Meanwhile, Ramakrishna continued…*)

You talk of worshipping idols. Why not? There are different staircases which lead to the truth. One can take the stairs he chooses to. The end justifies the method taken to achieve it.

But how can we bring our mind to focus on God?

What you need is concentration that comes from meditation and good company. Like a sapling when planted needs to be tended to with care till it becomes a tree, so too the mind must be guarded well against countless distractions that come with our association with worldly matters. So, good company is essential.

Is it possible to see God? In which state of mind can one become one with God?

Yes, indeed. As clearly we can see each other. But as one yearns for money and for family, the same extreme desire must pervade the mind of the devotee to see God.

(Mahendranath, by now, had understood the import of what had been said by the Master).

In the context of belief, someone asked Ramakrishna which was superior: devotion laced with love or devotion inspired by knowledge? "Both are important," said Ramakrishna. "Knowledge is important to know about God, just as love is integral to becoming one with Him." He told a story about three friends who come across a tiger while passing through a *jungle*. The first said, "Death is certain now." The second said, "Let's meditate. God will help us." The third said, "Why trouble God for such a small problem. Let's climb a tree and save our lives." The first was ignorant about God. The second had knowledge about God's will over life and death. The third loved God and did not want to trouble Him for a matter as small as this. So, Ramakrishna concluded, both knowledge and love are important and must converge to help one on the route to acquire God-consciousness.

Ramakrishna's message of 'Belief' transcended the barriers of gender and brought in scores of female devotees. His disciples like Yogi Maa, Golap Maa and Aghormani Devi never felt uncomfortable about the fact that their Guru was a male. Ramakrishna once related an anecdote. There was a revered Guru who always asked his disciples to steer clear of women, the farther, the better. One day, two of his disciples, one young and the other old were crossing a river when they saw a woman hesitating to cross the river due to fear. While the elderly disciple quietly crossed the river, the younger one lifted the woman on his shoulders and helped her cross the river. "Wait till I complain about this to the Master," said his companion. "What have I done?" asked the young disciple. "What you have done? You have disobeyed our master and touched a woman," said the other. The young disciple smiled, "I simply made a helpless woman sit on my shoulders and left her on the other side of the river. But as for you, she still seems to sit heavily on your mind." Man or woman, it's the way you think that determines your action, Ramakrishna used to say.

Coming to his female disciples, **Yogi Maa** was facing domestic turbulence despite being married to an affluent person. Her anxieties seemed to melt away the moment Ramakrishna cast a glance at her. The decision was taken forthright: she was to spend the rest of her life in Dakhineshwar in service of the Mother.

Golap Maa was a hapless widow from a middle-class background whose daughter had passed away. She was shattered and life became so vacuous to her. She had heard about Yogi Maa and decided to go to Ramakrishna. She too was destined to spend her life serving Maa Kali.

Aghormani Devi was 60 when she first met Ramakrishna in 1884. She had taken some sweets along with her. The moment Ramakrishna set her eyes on her, he said, "Why don't you give me the sweets you've brought for me?" He ate the sweets with utmost glee and then said, "But why waste money? You can make sweets with coconuts at home," after which he gave a detailed recipe of a wide variety of home-made sweets. This put Aghormani Devi in a quandary. What sort of ascetic is he who talks so greedily of sweets? Has she come to the right place?

Some time passed before she came back, this time with home-made sweets. Ramakrishna again ate them to his heart's content. This time, Aghormani saw Gopala in Ramakrishna. She felt as if it was Gopala devouring the sweets and not Ramakrishna. Her guards fell, all her suspicions were dispelled and she became a *bhakt* for the rest of her life.

Not only men and women, Ramakrishna attached great importance to the youth being initiated on the path of spirituality. "I am merely the initiator," he used to say, "It's the youth who will lead the way to the ultimate truth." He was proud he had a battery of young *Turks* as his disciples. When a young disciple asked him if it is proper to get married while trying to know God, Ramakrishna said, "One should try not to. But it's better to get married than repent not tasting the marital soup for the entire life as this could dent your concentration. In fact, to know the hassles involved with conjugal life, one ought to get married." Ramakrishna was never averse to the idea of the company of women. When he heard about one of his disciples, Harinath who did not even look at women in the eye, he mildly chided him, saying, "A woman is a reflection of the Mother. By not looking at her, you are insulting her. Change your mindset. Look at a woman the way you see the Mother and your mind will be at ease."

❑

9

The Last Days

"Disease is the tax which the soul pays for the body, as a tenant pays rent for a house."

The year: 1885. Ramakrishna suffered from clergyman's throat, which gradually developed into throat cancer. He was moved to Shyamapukur near Kolkata, where some of the best physicians of the time, including Dr Mahendralal Sarkar, treated him. When his condition aggravated he was relocated to a large garden house at Cossipore. Ramakrishna knew he was dying. It had become impossible for him to even drink water.

Even while facing the pangs of impending death, Ramakrishna never lost his poise. Vivekananda once asked him, "Master, you can at least ask God to enable you to eat and drink. It's increasingly becoming difficult for your body to withstand the pain. We too are experiencing great anxiety. If you cannot eat, neither can we. If you cannot drink, neither can we. So if you don't care about yourself, at least think about us. Please ask God to do you this little favour."

Ramakrishna knew he couldn't hurt Vivekananda. He closed his eyes for a few seconds, opened them and started laughing. "You fool! If I listen to your advice God will laugh at me. I did ask him. God laughed at me and said, 'Ramakrishna, you are listening to these fools? You follow their advice? Are they your disciples or are you their disciple? Who is who? You have eaten with this throat for so many years - can't you now eat and drink with the throats of your disciples? God's argument appeals to me. So stop torturing yourself, because now that I have lost my throat, I have to depend on your throats. Eat as much as you can - a little more than usual, because a part of it has to go to me. Drink a little more than usual because there will be my share, too. So eat, drink and rejoice, because God has said so."

This is an example of supreme sacrifice as it is a corroboration of the fact that pain, as we put it, is all part of the body which is eminently perishable. Think less what the body will eat and more about the food for the soul which is imperishable. This was the beauty of Ramakrishna's logic, so real yet so convincingly put with a certain invisible power of uniting the master with his disciples.

As the end inched closer, Ramakrishna called Vivekananda and told him, "I leave my disciples to your care. See that they practise spiritual disciplines even after my passing away and they do not return home." Another day, he wrote on a piece of paper, "Narendra will teach people." When Vivekananda expressed unwillingness, Ramakrishna said: "But you must. Your very bones will do it." Vivekananda used to describe his Master's message to humanity thus:

> **"First build a strong character – that is the highest duty you can perform. Know truth for yourself, and there will be many to whom you can teach it afterwards. They will all come. This was the attitude of my Master. He criticised no one. For years I lived with that man, but never did I hear those lips utter one word of condemnation of any sect. I learned from my Master that the religions of the world are not contradictory or antagonistic. They are but various phases of one eternal religion."**

Narendra once narrated how Ramakrishna had transmitted his power into him: "Some days before his passing away, he called me to his side and looked steadily at me and went into a *samadhi*. Then I felt that a subtle force like an electric shock was entering my body. In a little while, I also lost outward consciousness and sat motionless. How long I stayed in that condition I do not remember. When my consciousness returned, I found my Master shedding tears. On questioning him, he replied affectionately: 'Today, having given you all I had, I have become a beggar. With this power you are to do much work for the good of the world before you return.' I feel that power is constantly directing me to do all my work. This body has not been made for remaining idle."

Three days before Ramakrishna's death, it became clear that the end was imminent soon, very soon. Sharda Maa was upset and could not control her tears. Ramakrishna gave her his childlike, beatific smile and said, "Why do you cry? Because the one who is, is not going to die. And did you love this body known as me or did you love the one who is?" Sharda Maa said, "I loved the one who is." Ramakrishna said, "Then stop worrying. Going by what you said, when he who is not, dies, do not break your bangles."

Ramakrishna attained *'mahasamadhi'* on August 16, 1886. Everybody else wept, but not Sharda Maa.

She did not break her bangles either. She remained the same as she always was. In those days, this was unheard of. Everybody clicked their tongue and said, "O my God!! What are you doing? Your husband is dead and you must break your bangles." Sharda Maa stubbornly defied all advice. "One who has died was not there in the first place and the one who was there, still is. These bangles are in his memory," she said. Sharda Maa remained a bride even after Ramakrishna's death. She never said that Ramakrishna was no more and whenever somebody asked, she would say, "That body had become worn and torn, he has only changed clothes."

That's the reality Ramakrishna wanted us to realise. The body is a cocoon we can dispense with. The soul is immortal. A week after Ramakrishna's death, Vivekananda suddenly saw a flash of dazzling light. He felt his Master was standing right there in front of him. The light gradually dimmed. Vivekananda knew his Master was and will always be by his side.

❑❑❑